Flora Drew

Ma Jian is the author of *Red Dust: A Path Through China,* which won the Thomas Cook Prize in the U.K., and the novel *Stick Out Your Tongue.* He lives in England.

ALSO BY MA JIAN

Red Dust: A Path Through China

Stick Out Your Tongue

International Praise for *The Noodle Maker*

"*The Noodle Maker* is beautifully translated from the Chinese. . . .
These are surrealistic and often bawdy, with a frankness that veers
from clinical to crude."

—*The Independent* (U.K.)

"Clever and humorous . . . Constructed with a good deal of
artfulness . . . Fans of the absurdity and dark humor of Milan
Kundera's portraits of life behind the Iron Curtain will appreciate these same elements in Ma Jian's work."

—*The Baltimore Sun*

"Succinct and right on target . . . Blistering satire."

—*Kirkus Reviews*

"In *Red Dust,* Ma Jian gave us a dazzling portrait of life for a
dissident in China. *The Noodle Maker* is an even greater accom-
plishment. Playful and wonderfully dark, it confirms Jian as a
Chinese Kundera or Mrozek or Gogol. The funniest book I've
read in a long time."

—Philip Marsden, author of *The Bronski House*

"A brilliant and disturbing novel, portraying cruel, heartless deeds
and a frustrated and angry people stamped down by rigid state
control. In lesser hands this would all be too much, but Jian is a
born storyteller, spinning tales with an almost fablelike quality. It
is a most compelling read—a book I shall not forget in a hurry."

—*Publishing News* (London)

"These stories reflect the changing repressive conditions of modern China. . . . Two friends tell each other absurd stories in which
a strange cast of characters negotiate the narrow space between
party rules and criminal 'bourgeois liberalism.'"

—*The Boston Globe*

MA JIAN

The Noodle Maker

Translated from the Chinese by Flora Drew

Picador

Farrar, Straus and Giroux

New York

For information on Picador Reading Group Guides, as well as ordering, please contact Picador.
Phone: 646-307-5629
Fax: 212-253-9627
E-mail: readinggroupguides@picadorusa.com

ISBN 0-312-42479-5
EAN 978-0-312-42479-4

Originally published in 1991 by Tiandi Publishing Company, Hong Kong, as
Lamianzhe

English translation originally published in 2004 by Chatto and Windus, Great Britain

First published in the United States by Farrar, Straus and Giroux

P1

For Jack Ma

Contents

The Noodle Maker

The Professional Writer

The study faces a kitchen window of the opposite building. At midday or dusk, 'waves of delicious frying smells stroke or sometimes blast their way through my nose and stomach'. The professional writer always speaks with this level of precision during his conversations with the professional blood donor.

The writer can now distinguish smells from at least three of the kitchens below. Living at the top of an eight-floor building as he does, he has no choice but to get used to them. As long as the couple from Hubei (he's convinced they are the culprits) are not fouling the air with their fried chillies, he can sit back and enjoy the smells that waft up from several floors below. Whenever he pushes his window open to let the smells in, his eyes drift from the blank manuscript paper on his desk, and he sinks into a trance.

The kitchen directly opposite him is very much to his taste, and if he's not feeling too particular, he can spend an entire afternoon luxuriating in the fragrance of their fish-head soup. He's seen those large fish heads in the market; you only need buy half a head to make a pot of soup. As the middle-aged woman in the kitchen opposite tosses the Superior Dried Mushrooms, fresh from the local supermarket, into the wok, the professional writer (forties, slightly overweight, single) is overcome once more by the sweet aromas. Now and then, in the dim light, he glimpses a short little man appearing and disappearing between the kitchen implements and washing-up cloths, sausages and prime joints of ham that hang from the ceiling. If their smoke extractor were not making such a racket, he'd be able to hear them talk, and then he could find out at last whether the short little man is her husband,

3

her son, or a Jewish trader from Chaozhou. This question often flits through his mind when he stares down at the blank page on his desk. Before his good friend the professional blood donor arrives today, he spits furious insults at the kitchen. 'Ginger!' he mutters impatiently. 'Fucking idiots! Don't you know you have to put ginger in fish-head soup?'

Later that Sunday afternoon, the blood donor turns up at the writer's apartment block as usual. Listening to him plod and pant up the stairwell, the writer can tell that his friend has just given blood. The donor is indeed as happy as a poet as he struggles up the stairs, for today he's brought with him wine (it's usually a bottle of Anhui or Hubei medicinal wine), roast goose, eggs (real brown eggs) and the writer's favourite delicacy: a jar of spicy broad beans. Soon the friends will swig back the wine and start to rummage through the fragments of their lives. They will pour their hearts out to each other, insult and curse each other, while all the time savouring the pleasant sensation of food rubbing into their stomachs. Then the blood donor will try to provoke the writer into swearing at him. He loves to hear him swear; the foul language offers him a spiritual comfort sorely lacking in a life lived through giving blood.

'For fuck's sake!' he will hear the writer moan as the alcohol drifts to his head. 'You're wasting your time on those fucking losers, you miserable bastard . . .'

The writer opens his door to let the blood donor in. After a brisk embrace, they arrange the food on plates, open the bottle of wine, and spread out sheets of manuscript paper for the discarded bones. The writer then carefully tears a sheet of paper in half to make two napkins: one for his hands, the other for his mouth. (His grandfather did the same when he was alive, but used a piece of old cloth instead.) They take their seats at the table. The writer squeezes into his state-allotted black leather revolving chair, the professional blood donor perches on a plastic stool.

'Are you suffering, my friend?' the blood donor asks, hoping to lure the writer out of his shell. 'Last week you said that life was hell. Am I right?'

'Last year I thought life was hell. Last week I thought it was unbearable. Today I just think it's a bore. Maybe tomorrow I'll give up on this damn novel, if I still can't manage to put these characters onto the page.' The professional writer's voice is always hoarse before the wine starts to take effect. It sounds as though he is putting it on.

'But you hate those people! You said they're dregs, worthless trash. You said I was the scum of the earth too. Why waste your time writing about them?' The blood donor's face is as pale as it was when he first entered the room.

'I want to transform their lives into a work of art, although I'm sure they will never bother to read it.' The writer glances around the room, or perhaps he's just moving his head. 'Stupid bastards!' he grumbles. 'They always forget to put ginger in their fish-head soup.'

The Professional Blood Donor

Without waiting to raise his glass for a toast, the blood donor grabs the fattest chunk of goose (buttock, perhaps) between his chopsticks, and pops it into his mouth. Being a blood donor by profession, he has developed an instinctive capacity to pick out the most nutritious food on the table. He can extract every drop of goodness from each chunk of food, then chew it down to its last scrap.

'You have a very acute sense of smell,' the blood donor says, swallowing his first mouthful.

'I don't understand those two,' the writer mutters. 'They keep dashing about in a terrible hurry. They must have a lot to do.'

'I've been at it for seven years now.' The blood donor spits out a shard of broken bone. A dark glob of blood falls from the marrow and congeals on the white paper.

'So have I,' the professional writer replies, chomping on his chunk of goose. As he chews voraciously and throws his head back to swallow, the rolls of middle-aged fat under his chin squeeze in and out. From a distance, it looks as though he's weeping. The blood donor knows that the writer's face will soon assume the form of a swollen walnut, as it always does when the alcohol starts to kick in.

'I don't have to tax my brain to get this food on the table,' the blood donor says provocatively. 'Still, I have a lot of pain in here,' he adds, patting his chest. He has used this last phrase many times over the past seven years. He picked it up from the writer. After the donor's second blood donation, the writer took him in his arms and sobbed, 'I have a lot of pain in here.'

'You must add thin slices of ginger to fish-head soup to take away the bitter aftertaste. Everyone knows that!' The writer lowers his head and spews out a broken bone onto the manuscript paper. 'My book is going nowhere. I'll have to start again from scratch.'

The donor stares at the writer's balding crown: thin strands of wisdom springing from a shiny scalp.

The blood donor is known as Vlazerim, a nickname he acquired during the Cultural Revolution when he, the writer and their fellow 'urban youths' were sent to a re-education camp in the countryside to 'learn from the peasants'. Vlazerim is the swarthy hero of an Albanian propaganda film. The night after his production team were shown the film, he shouted from his sleep, 'Hey, Vlazerim!' and the name has stuck to him ever since. Unfortunately, he is not as tall and strong as the hero of the film. When the Cultural Revolution came to an end, he returned to this town and tried to look for a job, but since he had no particular skills or backdoor connections, he had difficulty finding suitable employment. After two years of living on the streets, he finally picked up a job in the Western District, dredging excrement from the public latrines. Unfortunately, no one told him that when you lug shit about, you have to balance a plank of wood over the top of the bucket to stop it tipping over. However hard he tried, he never managed to wash the stench from his trousers, and ended up selling them to a peasant for one and a half yuan.

Then one day he joined the crowded ranks of the town's blood donors, and for the first time in his life, received forty-five yuan's worth of food rations, a doctor's authorisation to buy pig liver, and coupons for three kilograms of eggs. Everything he could ever have hoped for in life was granted to him in a single day. When he returned home and whacked the doctor's authorisation and ration coupons onto the table, his parents and elder sister suddenly saw him in a new light. He soon took over as head of the family. When he was awarded a coupon to buy a Phoenix bicycle for helping a textile factory with its donation quotas, his fame spread throughout the district. Neighbours gathered at his home to chat about his latest successes. Three large factories in the Western District issued him with fake identity papers so that he could donate blood on behalf of their staff. Smaller work units tried to bribe him with wine and cigarettes, hoping he would help them out as well, but he could never be bothered to stick his neck out for them.

After seven years of hard work, Vlazerim is now a millionaire. His pockets are stuffed with awards and prizes from government factories and private enterprises. He has coupons to buy electric fans, televisions, matches, coal, gas and meat. A few years ago, he and a couple of friends set up a Blood Donor Recruitment Agency in a public latrine in the middle of town. They position their desk in the yard next to a pool of urine, and place a plank between the desk and the puddle to protect them from stray splashes. At night they lock the desk to the railings with a metal chain so that no one can take it away. They pay just three yuan a month in rent to the local hygiene board, the only restriction on their business being that they are forbidden to put up a signboard. Most days they are able to pull ten or twenty people off the street and persuade them to join the agency. When the new recruits have finished with the formalities, they walk to the hospital across the road to give blood, then return to the latrine, hand over to the agency half the cash they've earned, and take home the rest. The blood donor splits the profit with his colleagues, but always keeps the largest share for himself.

The agency is equipped with all the materials and documents necessary for giving blood. They have piles of paper, official stamps, glue, forged identity cards and passport photographs. If the recruit is underweight, the agency can fill his stomach with drinking water, or attach heavy metal rods to his legs. If the recruit is too short, the agency has four pairs of high-heeled shoes in differing sizes that they lend out free of charge. (A man stole two pairs from them once when they weren't looking. They had heels three centimetres high – enough for a child of twelve to pass the hospital's minimum height requirements for prospective donors.)

The friends suck and chew the meat, mashing it to a soft pulp.

Outside, everything has turned dark blue. It is the dim, blurry scene that follows sunset. There are lights shining in the high-rise buildings; from the window it looks like a starry night sky.

The two men chomp and swallow the food, savouring each mouthful. Their voices are beginning to sound tired.

This dinner cost twice as much as the professional writer's monthly wage. It's a proper meal with real meat. The writer ate very little meat as a child. His mother was only able to make soup if he and his brothers happened to pick up a scrap of pork rind on the streets. The blood donor's background was more privileged. In the re-education camp he boasted that he'd eaten meat seventeen times in his life. But after just one year of giving blood, he could afford to eat twice this amount. Premier Deng Xiaoping's strategy of opening the country to the outside world and introducing economic reform had set him walking on the road to paradise.

'In the re-education camp, we were only given meat once,' the blood donor says. 'I remember the night before it was served. I lay in bed, unable to sleep. I hadn't eaten a thing all day. The cook was in the kitchen frying the meat, and the smells were wafting all the way up to our dormitory.'

'I used to worship Gorky at the time,' the writer says. 'I also liked those books by Gogol and Hans Andersen that the authorities confiscated from the county library.'

'You're looking rough these days. I bet you haven't left your flat all week.' The blood donor exhales a puff of tobacco. He can buy six packs of foreign cigarettes for one television coupon. 'Tell me,' he says. 'Am I looking yellow and thin?'

'Just the opposite. You look green and fat.' The writer opens his electric kettle and watches the eggs boiling away inside. One of the shells has broken, and a strand of yolk is wriggling through the water like a fish. 'Ha! There's a disaster looming,' he mumbles distractedly, remembering the plot of a fable he read the day before. 'Look at this cracked shell. The sailors are shipwrecked and the king is on the run . . .' His face looks even more like a walnut now, although he appears to be smiling. It must be the alcohol swilling through his stomach.

The Party secretary of the local Writers' Association called him in recently to assign him a new task. He announced that the Party's Central Committee had decided that the national campaign to learn from Lei Feng – the selfless PLA soldier who dedicated his life to serving the revolutionary cause and the needs of the common people – was due to reach a peak in March. The secretary commissioned the writer to compose a short novel on the theme of 'Learning from Comrade Lei Feng'.

'Find me a modern Lei Feng,' the secretary said. 'Someone in today's world who has the same socialist consciousness that Lei Feng had in the 1960s. "Seek truth from the facts", as our Premier says. Make him come alive on the page, and finish the story with him losing his life while trying to save a comrade in distress.'

The professional writer felt faint as he sat opposite his leader. He tried to keep his eyes open and force out a smile. He knew that this was the expression expected of him.

'In which year did Lei Feng die?' the writer asked. He knew very well the answer to the question; he just wanted to give his leader a chance to scold him.

'Do you really need to ask me that? You'd better think things through, Comrade Sheng. You have obviously not taken Lei Feng into your heart.'

'The Party is in my heart,' the writer said.

'Hmm. Well, now you have a chance to prove that to us. The Party has trained you to wield your pen, and now is your opportunity to wield it. Do you understand? "For a thousand days we train our troops, to use them in just one battle", as the saying goes. It's time you paid back your debts to the Party. I'll leave the details to you. Come and see me if there are any problems. But let me warn you, your work was not up to scratch last year. The titles and contents of your stories were poor, and the political standpoint of the reformers was ambiguous. You should not have placed the senior Party cadres in the roles of the reactionaries.'

'Last year the newspapers reported that the senior cadres were too conservative, and that the Party wanted them to loosen their reins and let the younger cadres take control of the reform process.'

'Well this year it's changed, hasn't it? Now it's the older you are, the more reformist you are. "The waves of the Yangtze River are pushed forward from behind", as the saying goes.'

'What age should I make my Lei Feng?' the writer asked, pulling out his notebook.

The secretary paused for a while. 'You'll have to decide that yourself. But don't take too long. As we speak, every writers' association in the country is preparing for this campaign. They're putting their best writers on the job. Make sure you don't miss the boat.' Then he stopped and looked him straight in the eye. 'If you come up with a good story about a new Lei Feng, the Party organs will send you an application form for inclusion in *The Great Dictionary of Chinese Writers*.'

'My very own place in history!' the writer exclaims to his friend. 'Just one short novel, and I can enter *The Great Dictionary of Chinese Writers*.'

The donor nods his head. 'You will become immortal.'

'I must find a living Lei Feng, but I can't think of anyone suitable.' The writer remembers taking out his diary on his first day in the re-education camp, and writing on the front page: 'Just like Lei Feng, I will be a screw that never rusts. Wherever the Party chooses to place me, I will shine.' He remembers learning how Lei Feng wore the same pair of socks for five years, darning them again and again, preferring to give his money away to the poor rather than buy himself a new pair. The writer racks his brain, trying to think of someone he knows who shows the same selfless, heroic qualities, but all that comes to mind are the characters of his unwritten novel: a young entrepreneur who runs a private crematorium; an illegal migrant who writes letters for the illiterate; a father who spends his life trying to get rid of his retarded daughter . . .

These are people he knows, has read about or sees every day on the streets. They are the people he understands, the people he'd write about, if he had the courage. Their lives are as miserable and constricted as his own. But he is fully aware that if he wrote about these sad and feeble characters, his leaders would consider him unfit for the post of professional writer. He would lose his state salary, his apartment, his membership of the Writers' Association, and any chance of being included in the literary encyclopaedias.

The chunks of goose meat are enjoying a gentle massage by their stomachs' digestive juices. The friends seem more at ease now.

'The eggs are ready,' the blood donor says. 'You will enter *The Great Dictionary*. You're a writer, the conscience of our generation. But look at me! I've saved hundreds of lives by giving blood, but what have I got to show for it? I could die tomorrow and no one would know. Unless you decide to write about me, of course.'

'Your profession is despicable. It's degenerate. It proves that human nature is essentially evil.'

'Roast goose doesn't grow on trees, you know.' The blood donor points to the pieces of spat-out bone stuck to the manuscript paper. 'If it weren't for me, the national blood banks would be empty. I've bled myself dry for this country.'

'They still haven't put any ginger in their fish-head soup,' the writer grumbles.

'If it weren't for me, this country would be finished!'

'Foreigners give blood for free,' the writer retorts. 'You're a fraud, a fake philanthropist.'

'I'm more real than you are,' the blood donor snaps, touching a nerve. Over the years, he has slowly learned to speak the writer's language, and knows where to insert his knife.

'The king is in trouble now!' the writer chuckles to himself, leaning back in his chair. 'The sailors are clambering to shore . . .'

'The factory leaders depend on us to fulfil their blood donation quotas. If their own employees gave blood, they'd have to fork out thousands of yuan a year on sick pay and convalescent breaks. We only take cash, and we've never asked for a convalescent break. Many factories have been granted the status of "advanced enterprises" because of the blood we've given on their behalf. Well, I'm an "advanced blood donor", a selfless Lei Feng devoted to the cause of the people. You say foreigners give blood for free. Well, if the government could be bothered to give me a proper job, I would give blood for free too.'

The writer's jaw drops. 'You – a living Lei Feng! All right then, I'll write about you. The blood-donating saviour of the people. The new Lei Feng. But the trouble is – you make money out of it . . .'

'So what?' the blood donor says, unwilling to let slip this chance to achieve fame. 'I'm more Lei Feng than Lei Feng! If you write about me, you won't have to bother to "Go Down among the Masses" or to "Learn about Life through Personal Experience". I gave blood twice in one day to help out a man who had been ordered to give blood by the Party. Not even Lei Feng would have done that. And as for all the other good deeds I've done in my past, well you know about them already.' He snatches the bottle of medicinal wine from the centre of the table, pours out a few drops for the writer, and empties the rest into his own glass. Then he gets up from the table and goes to fetch a box of matches. 'You always promised you would write about me,' he says, lighting a cigarette. 'I would have given up this job ages ago otherwise.'

'Do you know anything about the brain?' the writer asks blankly. 'My thoughts seem to arrive in unconnected paragraphs. They never connect. They set up home in my mind and pour their hearts out. They couldn't care less about me, but I depend on them for my livelihood. You, though, have always been rooted to the real world, and over the years, you've influenced me and brought me down to earth. Who knows? Tomorrow I might just start giving blood myself. But I . . .' The writer takes a drag from his cigarette, and glances at the blood donor sitting opposite him. '. . . I've influenced you too. You've taken every word of criticism I've used against you in the past, and now you're using them against me. Maybe you're the one who's going to end up in the history books. You and your lot.'

'I don't eat much these days,' the blood donor says. 'It takes me twice as long to climb the stairs now. My movements are clumsy.'

'You're in better shape than I am. In the re-education camp, you were the pasty one. Always playing sick, lying in bed while the rest of us were out working.' A sour tone has crept into the writer's voice, as it always does when the first bottle of wine is finished. My mind is filled with stories, he thinks to himself. But I have no idea how to piece them together. I need to be with people. I need to go out and speak to people before I can reach any deeper understanding.

'You swallow jugfuls of water before giving blood,' the writer adds, after a long pause. 'You could harm someone that way.'

'I've only done that once. What others get up to is their own business. Most of the recruits tie metal rods to their legs these days.'

'You've never really grown up.'

The blood donor stares at the writer's face, trying to assess the seriousness of the remark. But the writer's eyes are hidden behind his glasses, and there is no emotion in his voice.

'You are utterly self-centred,' the writer continues. 'You never pay attention to the world around you.' Reaching for a second bottle of wine, he thinks to himself: As far as he and I are concerned, Lei Feng is a dead man, like any other. Everyone is equal in death. What's the difference between General Cao Cao, Marshal Liu Bei, and Comrade Lei Feng? They're just a bunch of dead men, that's all . . .

The blood donor looks at the writer's mouth, then at his ears. He knows that it's his mouth that draws him to this room. In the re-education camp, he and the other urban youths would sit around the writer and stare at his mouth, waiting to hear what would come out of it.

'Could you ever be entirely selfless and devote yourself to the people?' the writer asks with a sneer. His question seems to be directed at both himself and the blood donor.

'I refuse to be anyone's slave. The constitution states that all men are equal, so why should I put myself down and sacrifice myself to others?' The blood donor has dropped his obsequious tone. He has clearly given up trying to persuade his friend to write about him.

The writer remains silent. He knows that his life is almost entirely devoted to the Party. But he has no idea who the Party is. He knows that the Party was around before he was born, and has controlled him his entire life. Every part of him belongs to the Party. The Party told him to write novels. It could tell him to die too if it wanted – he'd have no choice in the matter. Vlazerim exchanges his blood for food, he exchanges his mind instead. He remembers how the blood donor looked as he gobbled the roast goose: his entire body consumed in the act of eating, his mind focused on the need to eat, the need to survive. When he bit into the chunk of goose breast, a blob of grease dripped down his shirt and fell onto the table.

'You're a beast,' the writer replies, peeling the shell from a steaming-hot egg.

The blood donor shoots him a disparaging look. 'When we were sent to the countryside, you talked about the "Sublime". You even went on about that man Jesus. But now look at you! You've spent the whole day just waiting for me to turn up and put meat on your table. You can't buy much food with the money they pay you for your deep thoughts, can you?' The blood donor grabs an egg then pushes the plate back towards the bottles in the middle of the table. He takes a pinch of salt from the jar beside him, removes the hot shell and rubs the salt onto the gleaming white surface of the egg. 'I get three times your monthly salary for just one blood donation. When you look at what you put into your work and what you get out of it, you're not doing too well, are you? Or to put it another way, just because I'm a professional blood donor and you're a professional writer doesn't mean you're any better than me.'

The writer stares in disgust at the blood donor's mouth, at the egg yolk moving inside it. He often adopts this disapproving look when his stomach is full. 'If everyone were like you,' he says, 'this country would be ruined.'

'Don't be so sure. You're a blood donor yourself. The reason

I'm better off than you is because my blood saves lives, and earns me money and respect. But what have you got for your sweat and blood, for all that expended grey matter? Nothing. Your salary is only just enough to keep you breathing. You depend on the smell of your neighbours' cooking to get you through the day. What kind of life is that? You talk about God, and your need to find the truth, but what help has your God ever been to you?'

'You're only interested in food. What do you know about truth?' The writer's expression is now calm and composed. 'I will spend the rest of my life in quiet meditation. The sages live on one meal a day, the average man on two. I will survive on . . .'

'Everyone needs three square meals a day.'

'Only animals eat three meals a day,' the writer says with conviction. 'I'm not fussy about what I eat. We didn't have fish-head soup tonight, but I didn't kick up a fuss, did I?'

'In fact three meals a day aren't nearly enough for me. What does that make me then?'

'A beast,' the writer replies. He inhales a gust of fragrant air, and says to himself: That smells like smoked mushrooms. Maybe if you add them to fish-head soup you can leave out the ginger. 'You live off your body fluids,' he continues, 'so you must be a beast.'

'If you don't start eating properly, you'll turn into a lump of dried tofu.' The blood donor observes the writer's hunched shoulders and his sallow, palsied face. 'Very soon, you will weigh less than a sheet of manuscript paper, and then you will disappear altogether.'

The blood donor's eyes sparkle with life, in stark contrast to the writer, whose energies are slowly failing him and who has lost the will to write. The blood donor's face is free of wrinkles and flushed with blood. His thick lips are moist and red. No one would guess he gives blood on a weekly basis, unless they heard him faltering up the stairs. His small, narrow body seethes with fresh young blood and gastric juices. At mealtimes he can finish every scrap of food on the table. Before he gives blood, he can swallow two thermos flasks of water and keep it all in for half an hour without having to relieve himself. His body is a blood-making machine, every part in fine working order.

The writer, however, has a weak heart, and a troublesome pair of lungs which spew out globs of phlegm at inopportune moments. None of the organs below his stomach are quite right either. He has to rush to the toilet as soon as any food reaches his intestines. Years of sitting at a desk have contorted his guts, causing him to suffer from perennial haemorrhoids. His feeble kidneys absolved him from having to take part in the Writers' Association's annual blood donation, and although his liver is now behaving reasonably well, it was nearly the death of him during his years in the camp.

But despite his relentless blood donations, Vlazerim is looking more suave and relaxed by the day. He doesn't have to tax his brains, so never experiences the dizziness, insomnia and disturbing dreams the writer suffers from – the afflictions of intellectuals. His imagination is only engaged when he's day-dreaming about recipes. During his time in the re-education camp, he stole a chicken once and took it up into the hills. He rubbed it with spices, roasted it over a wooden fire and gobbled it down all by himself. When he was finished, he buried the feathers in the ground. Had the guard dogs not sniffed out those feathers and dug them up, he would have got away with his crime without a beating.

Now, every organ in his body is focused on the pleasure of his masticating jaws.

'I'm no victim,' the blood donor says. 'Deng Xiaoping's Open Door Policy has rescued me, and allowed me to create a new life for myself. All my misery vanished the day they first gave me money for my blood. Now I have everything I want. But you're still stuck here, wallowing in self-pity, yearning for the day you'll make it into *The Great Dictionary of Chinese Writers*. You hate yourself for writing what the Party tells you to write. You mystify life, so that you can rationalise your loss of grip on reality. You've forgotten that man survives through his quest for profit, not truth. Without the profit motive, we would all be finished. In the end, everyone gets what they deserve.'

'You could be an intellectual yourself, if you wanted,' the writer laughs. His mind starts to drift again. What am I doing here? he asks himself. I have to find a new Lei Feng, make it into *The Great Dictionary of Chinese Writers* . . . But all I can see is the entrepreneur's face, the young man who runs the crematorium, who looks nothing like the boy he once was. I have been observing the world through his eyes for a while now. It's time he came and set fire to me too . . .

The Swooner

After he shut the steel door, everything went quiet.

He switched off the cassette player, stood up and examined the furnace's thermograph. '1,700 degrees,' he said, moving his nose closer to the furnace. 'Not burned to the bone yet.' At this stage, if the wind were blowing in the wrong direction, smells of roast flesh would fill the air and he would feel a pang of hunger. Ten minutes later, the delicious smells would be replaced by a sickening stench.

He had bought the large furnace off the ceramic department of the local art school. The students there no longer used it for their projects, and had dumped it in the yard of a local pottery factory. After his purchase was finalised, he transported the furnace from the yard to a small plot of land he rented from a peasant in the outskirts of town. Once the furnace was in place, he gave the exterior a lick of heat-resistant paint, replaced a few of the fire-proof bricks that lined the inside, and installed a new electric heating element. After he secured an entrepreneur's licence, he was able to use the beautiful kiln to reduce a total of one-hundred-and-nine cadavers to ashes.

His death register was filled with a list of names, each accompanied by a photograph, ready for the police to inspect. Of the dead, forty-nine were victims of car accidents; twenty had committed suicide by a range of methods including hanging, swallowing pesticides, inhaling carbon monoxide, and severing arteries. One man had even swallowed a kilogram of iron nails. There were Beijing opera stars and suburban farmers. The woman who had gassed herself with carbon monoxide was the daughter of a senior cadre – ordinary people in this town can't afford gas ovens. Glancing down the column headed 'educational background', you could see there were three university students (including the boy from the top university who was burning away right now), and thirty poets (this is not surprising – there are more poets in this town than prostitutes or rubbish collectors). The youngest fatality was a one-year-old baby who had fallen from the top of a building. She was a sweet little corpse, and only needed a third of the usual electricity requirement.

When the fifty-third corpse was cremated, the furnace's fireproof window shattered. The entrepreneur couldn't afford to replace the window, so he blocked it up with bricks. After that, he could no longer enjoy the sight of bodies being consumed by the flames, and had to rely on his experience to judge the correct timing. He always gave an extra seven minutes to anyone over the standard one-hundred-and-thirty kilogram weight, at no additional cost.

His crematorium had several advantages over the state-run incinerators. First, the corpses could enter the flames while swooning to the sound of their favourite piece of music. The entrepreneur could provide them with any music they requested, including all the unwholesome tunes that were banned by the Party. If the deceased had grown up in the 1930s, he would play the decadent songs 'When Will My Prince Come Back?' or 'Pretty Girls in Peach Blossom River'.

Admittedly, his prices were higher than the public crematoriums. He had to pay electricity bills and taxes, after all. But the dead were guaranteed a same-day burning. With state-run operations, the body waited at least a week for a cremation, over two weeks if it hit a busy period. Relatives had to pay for the body storage, and were often reduced to slipping backhanders to officials in an attempt to speed the process up. When these additional costs were taken into account, the crematorium worked out as quite good value. But the greatest advantage of choosing the Swooners' Crematorium, as the entrepreneur called it, was that the company sent a car to collect the body from the house, saving the family the trouble of finding their own transport. The relatives of the deceased could set up a modest wake at home, dispatch someone to the crematorium's liaison office in the centre of town to sort out the formalities, and that was it. When the body was collected later in the day the relatives could shed a few tears, then return to their lives as normal. With state-run operations, the proceedings dragged on so long that the relatives were almost reduced to corpses themselves.

The liaison office of the Swooners' Crematorium was a long narrow shed built in the entrance passage of an old building in the centre of town. The relatives visited the office to register the death, plan the cremation and buy the clothes and daily necessities the deceased would require in the Land of the Dead. The entrepreneur lived in this office with his mother. They were a great team. Their business flourished. Although his mother had very little knowledge of electricity (the entrepreneur was an electrician by trade), she knew all there was to know about the dead. They only saw each other at night. During the day, the mother looked after business in the office while the son travelled to the crematorium in the suburbs to deal with the dead bodies. He left the office at nine in the morning, and was rarely back before midnight.

At night, the two colleagues would meet in the long shed that occupied half the entrance passage of the building. When the son returned, the mother would sit on the bed sorting out the burial clothes he had retrieved from the bodies, and listen to what he had to say.

'Women burn more easily,' he told her one night. 'For someone as skinny as you, eight hundred degrees would be enough to get your flesh to fall from the bone.'

'What do you mean, fall from the bone?' she asked, glancing at the walls whose lower halves were painted pink – a colour that had only been available in the shops since the launch of the Open Door Policy.

'It's just like when you cook spare-ribs. When the temperature is high enough, the flesh just falls from the bone.'

'I think my leg is rotting. I should have cut out this boil long ago.' The mother's shadow on the pink wall behind her looked like a creature from another planet. 'You got your bones from me and your flesh from your father,' she said, lowering her gaze. She always avoided looking her son in the eye.

'That's why I'm so short,' he replied.

'It's your father's fault you can't find a woman. He had an unlucky face.'

'I know a lot about women,' the entrepreneur said indignantly. 'Most of them like to listen to piano music before they go into the oven.'

'What do men like to listen to?' The mother snatched a piece of old cloth she spotted lying on the corner of the bed, then folded it neatly and returned it to its place.

'Symphonies.' The son swung his bony legs. 'Men are tough brutes. Only strong, powerful music can send them into a swoon.'

'Men are animals. Don't waste your time playing music to them,' the mother snarled, reaching for a pair of dark woollen trousers.

'Everyone needs to swoon before they go.' All the neighbours knew that the entrepreneur was a great lover of music. After the Open Door Policy was launched, he was the first man in town brave enough to walk down the streets swinging a cassette player in his hand. The entrepreneur jumped up from his seat and threw his hand in the air. His hand's shadow was moving too. 'I always make sure they swoon. I've heard that unless the dead swoon before they go, their souls won't rise to heaven and their bodies won't burn properly. Swooning allows them to vanish from this world for ever.'

The mother's shadow looked very dark against the clean pink wall. 'Look, here's another hole you've made,' she growled. Every object in the room was second-hand: the table, the sheets, every stitch of cloth on her body. She sat on the bed watching her son pace back and forth. The room was two metres by ten, and had an arched ceiling. In the light of the fire, she could see the traces of white ash, or ash-like substance, clinging like ghosts to the red bricks at the top of the walls. The entrance passage smelt as bad as a public bathhouse. Most of the stench came from the stall-holder who sold fermented bean curd outside the front gate. If their front door was left open during the day, the smells would flow straight in.

The office looked cheerful and festive when one glimpsed it from the street. There was always loud music playing, and large displays of paper flowers, paper shoes, imperial hats and Western suits and ties (the manufacture of which had only been permitted since the introduction of the Open Door Policy). The paper money, paper horses and paper flowers were brand new, but all the burial clothes were second-hand. The entrepreneur would never have been so wasteful as to send a body into the oven with its burial clothes still on. He would leave the clothes on the corpse until the last minute, in case the relatives turned up to bid a last goodbye, then he would carefully remove them, fold them up and bring them back to the office. His mother would howl in despair if she discovered he had inadvertently ripped the cloth or torn off a button. When she sold the burial clothes on to the next family, she was always generous enough to knock the price down a little.

From a distance (or from the town's highest clock tower), the long narrow shed looked as bright as an open eye. When he first set up business there, the entrepreneur invited the most talented artist in town, a member of the 'Wild Beast' school apparently, to paint a large mural along the shed's outside wall. He paid him fifty yuan for it. At first, the artist was reluctant to fix his art onto a wall: he believed that art and beauty were fluid concepts, and encompassed activities such as pissing, burping, spitting and fondling women and bottles of beer. But the entrepreneur was persistent, and at last persuaded him to paint a scene of a girl with golden hair burning to death to the sound of beautiful music. Instead of the metal tray, he painted her lying on an imported Western Dream mattress, and squiggled a few lines below to indicate an electric grill. One look at the girl's smile and softly protruding breasts (which exceeded the maximum cup-size allowed by the Open Door Policy's poster regulations) and you could die a happy man.

25

Unfortunately, the minute the artist put down his brush, a woman from the neighbourhood committee turned up with two policemen in tow. They ordered the artist to paint over the line of cleavage (a stroke of brown paint slightly darker than the surrounding flesh tone). Once the offending cleavage had become flat and uninviting, the artist was ordered to mask the girl's bare legs. The muslin skirt he painted over them seemed to satisfy the policemen, as it fell just below her knees. At the top left hand corner of the mural he had painted a skinny little god, China's Lord of the Sky, and without waiting to be asked, the 'Wild Beast' quickly daubed a white cloud over the god's penis, and painted two more under his feet for the sake of symmetry. Then, in the background, he added a crowd of representative workers, peasants, businessmen, students and soldiers rising to the heavens with big smiles on their faces. Among their ranks were a couple of 'Four Eyes' (otherwise known as intellectuals) who had been allowed back on the scene since the Open Door Policy. The artist filled the remaining blank spaces with pretty angels and beguiling devils – you could tell them apart by the horns. At the bottom of the picture stood the Lord of the Underworld, who held opposite duties to the Lord of the Sky. It was clear from the images that he was responsible for punishing the most serious category of criminal: counter-revolutionaries. He employed torture techniques borrowed from Christianity, Islam and Buddhism: drowning in boiling fat, being run over by a car, pecked to death by eagles and eaten alive by snakes. The entrepreneur's mother later stuck a pair of paper horses over this section to hide the gruesome scenes.

The old apartment building with the half-blocked entrance passage looked very similar to the August 1st Uprising Memorial Museum in Beijing (without the ornate portico and huge arched windows, of course). The decoration of the facade reflected the different stages of prosperity brought about by the recent reforms. A few well-off families had replaced their old wooden-cased windows with aluminium frames and tinted glass. A bureau head had even installed air-conditioning, a foreign machine that sucks out hot air and blows in cold. You could guess the wealth of each household by the style and condition of the clothes that hung from the windows on bamboo poles. Most of the rooms on the ground floor had been converted into shops. A poster of a foreign movie star was pasted to the window of the Comrade Lei Feng Hair Salon.

The mother crossed her legs and picked up a burial nightshirt. The smoke from the burning incense coil spiralled through the morbid stench. One shirt had been worn by three different corpses already, and you could still smell aftershave (probably French) on the collar. She searched the garment for imperfections as carefully as though she were inspecting her own body. Her nimble fingers laboured through the night, darning every hole and tear. By the morning the shirt was looking brand new again, folded up on the top shelf of the office.

There was one embroidered jacket still lying on the bed though. If the entrepreneur had been more astute, he might have guessed what use she had in mind for it.

(At this point in his thoughts, the professional writer exhales a deep breath and moves his gaze to the night sky. Colours always look more seductive in the dark, he says to himself, as he listens to the noises coming from inside and outside the lit-up windows. Since it is quieter than the daytime, you can hear pebbles bounce off the shoes of a passer-by, and children under a street lamp humming 'Learn from the Good Example of Comrade Lei Feng'. A bicycle bell rings out occasionally, then melts into the darkness. At this time of night, people become sad and mysterious creatures. It's only when they are cooking, resting or chatting that the flavour of life pours from the streets and drifts into every home. As long as there are no women quarrelling, people can stare at the stars, share a meal with some friends, or go out on a date . . .)

At dusk, the entrepreneur would start burning the bodies that had been collected during the day. He would work until midnight, then return home laden with clothes and belongings.

Sometimes he came back with gold teeth or pieces of jewellery. In the mornings he drove his army motorbike out of town through a string of houses that until recently had been a stretch of open field, to his crematorium in the suburbs, a simple shack he had built from the bricks of an abandoned chicken shed. An iron barrel welded to the rectangular metal roof served as the chimney. His two drivers would dump the corpses on the shack's cement floor or on one of the three stretchers. When the bodies entered the crematorium, they seemed as comfortable in their new surroundings as music lovers in a concert hall.

The entrepreneur always made sure that the bodies were collected on the day of registration. He understood how things work. If a dead person hangs around the house for more than three days, the relatives not only stop weeping, they begin to resent its presence. He also ensured that the ashes were returned to the family within the week. Any later and he knew he would get a very frosty reception at the swooners' homes.

Sometimes the relatives would visit the office in the centre of town (finding their way from the address at the top of the entrepreneur's invoice) to collect the ashes themselves. But the boxes seldom contained the swooner whose photograph was stuck to the lid. The entrepreneur often divided one corpse's ashes between several boxes. He was forced to cheat in this way if he was to guarantee a prompt delivery of the remains. Anyway, as far as he was concerned, one person's ashes were the same as the next's. His drivers drove a small second-hand Fiat whose sides were emblazoned with the bright text:

WE CARE FOR OTHERS, WE CARE FOR THE PARTY, WE CARE FOR OUR MOTHERLAND. WE CARE FOR THE CAUSE OF DOUBLING THE NATION'S PRODUCTION BY THE 21ST CENTURY. GO DOWN AMONG THE PEASANTS! GO TO THE BORDER AREAS! GO TO THE SWOONERS' CREMATORIUM!

On the boot of the car was a picture of a huge crowd of people standing on a globe the size of a football. The eye-catching slogan below read: UP WITH PRODUCTION! DOWN WITH POPULATION!

'I really love them – the dead are much nicer than the living,' the entrepreneur once said to some weeping relatives when he arrived to deliver the ashes.

'China has a population of 1.2 billion. If more people don't hurry up and die, our country will be finished,' he told another family. 'Anyway, it's not as if he was a hero of the revolution, is it?' he added, noticing the word 'proletarian' in the political class column of the dead man's form.

The entrepreneur's greatest talent was in recommending music for the deceased. He only had to glance at the profession, political class, age, sex and photograph on the form and he could select the appropriate music from his list. The price of each song had to rise, of course, in line with the inflation brought about by the Open Door Policy.

BEETHOVEN'S 'FIFTH SYMPHONY': 5 YUAN
CHOPIN'S 'NOCTURNE': 7 YUAN
(Suitable for young girls and poets)
TCHAIKOVSKY'S 'PATHETIQUE': 8 YUAN
(Karajan's latest recording)
POTTIER'S 'THE INTERNATIONALE': 1.5 YUAN
ORFF'S 'FORTUNE, EMPRESS OF THE WORLD': 2 YUAN
(On special offer. A popular choice for intellectuals)

There were also some more familiar tunes at only half a yuan a go. These included the old favourites 'Riverwater', 'The Moon Reflected in Two Ponds', 'No Communist Party, No New China,' as well as 'Young Cabbages', 'I Give My Life to the Party' and 'Learn from the Good Example of Comrade Lei Feng'. If the deceased was a member of the Young Pioneers, he would play 'There are Many Good Deeds to be Done on Sunday' free of charge.

If the relatives had trouble deciding what to choose from the list, the entrepreneur would stick his chin out, sidle up to them and whisper, 'I have some more tapes in reserve. But you will have to pay for them in Foreign Exchange Certificates.' This secret stash of music included tapes of English rock, American country music, erotic French disco music and the original Hong Kong recordings of the Taiwanese pop star, Deng Lijun. 'The central authorities have started to confiscate Deng Lijun tapes,' he told them authoritatively. 'Anyone found in possession of one will be given a five-year prison sentence and have their urban residency permit revoked.'

His customers often followed his recommendations. Some of them found it hard to reach a decision because they had very little idea about the dead person's musical tastes.

'Trust me,' he told one family. 'I can tell at a glance that your daughter would like "Star-Crossed Lovers" and "Mistress Meng Weeps on the Great Wall".'

'But she was still a virgin,' the relatives whispered.

The entrepreneur looked again at the photograph on the form. The woman was well into her forties.

'Well, you decide. I have "Ave Maria", or "Disco Music for Making Love". The musical styles are different, but they will both do the same job. You can send her off to the Old Man in the Sky in whatever manner you please.' Since the relatives had a low level of education, he used the term 'Old Man in the Sky' instead of 'God'.

'You can choose to give her a virgin's cremation, or not. It's up to you,' he added, smiling at them as smugly as a matchmaker at a wedding.

'She always wanted to join the Party,' the mother confessed with a sly smile.

'Wanting to join the Party and joining the Party are two quite different things.' As far as politics were concerned, the entrepreneur was mature beyond his years. 'But if you like, I can play "The Party has Given Me a New Lease of Life" and "Socialism is Good" and she will die with no regrets.'

Soon, news of the entrepreneur's excellent service spread throughout the town. People discovered that being dead was not much different from being alive.

A constant din boomed from the entrepreneur's shack. He

had bought the cassette player from the first batch of goods imported from Japan following the launch of the Open Door Policy. It had four speakers. He would always try to play the music the relatives had requested, if time allowed. But the only real audience were the stray dogs in the yard outside who were drawn to the shack by the smell of burning swooners. The hounds would lie on the ground and sunbathe, or riffle through the discarded burial clothes. Sometimes the delicious smells wafting from the shack drove them into a frenzy, and they would run about the yard, chasing each other's tails.

Occasionally the entrepreneur spent the night in the shack. We should examine his professional conduct and analyse his immoral behaviour. A thirty-year-old bachelor must have something to hide. The grief he feels at the sight of female corpses is most unnatural. If we practise our Qigong, and use our 'eye of wisdom' to observe him through the walls of his shack, we will see this self-appointed leader pace the room, then stop at the feet of a certain leading cadre and glare at him like a man about to avenge the death of his father. With his death register in his hand, he subjects each swooner to ruthless interrogation, pausing now and then to give them a sharp kick in the shins.

One day, he had lying at his feet: a policeman, the municipal Party secretary, the deputy head of the local housing department, a retired second-grade Party cadre and the chairwoman of the neighbourhood committee. Not one of them posed a threat to him though. They lay on the ground, next to the intellectual, the doctor and the pianist, and in one breath, the entrepreneur cursed the lot of them.

Everyone is equal in death. Had these important people known they were going to be abused in this way, they would have sorted the rascal out while they were still alive. But now the swooners could only lie back silently as he passed his final judgements on them. He swore at the cop for not observing the traffic regulations and for unjustly confiscating his motorbike licence. He cursed the deputy head of the housing department for failing to help him with his accommodation problems. 'You even wanted to have me thrown out of my shed in the entrance passage,' he hissed. He berated them for their corruption saying, 'I could have bought myself a villa in the country with all the money I wasted on your bribes.' Then he walked back to the deputy head of the housing department and kicked him in the stomach. 'You had the cheek to accuse my shed of spoiling the look of the city. But when the Albanian prime minister came here on his state visit, it was you who decided to cover the town with those huge ugly hoardings.'

The entrepreneur was settling old scores. The year the Albanian prime minister, Mr Shehu, was due to visit, the local government decided that the tatty buildings on the most important streets should be covered with hardboard and painted with a mural of a long row of neat houses. Shehu would be driving past in a flash, so an impression was all that was required. One of these hardboard fronts was attached to the apartment block in which the entrepreneur was living with his mother at the time. It blocked all the light and air from their flat. The windows of the hardboard fronts were spaced at five metre intervals, and as luck would have it, they missed their apartment and ended up on his neighbours' flat. The local government issued the neighbours with a length of curtain, and as long as they hung it up for the five minutes when Shehu's car was expected to pass, it was theirs to keep afterwards. The entrepreneur thought this was very unfair, as the neighbours' class origins were similar to his own – they both belonged to one of the 'Five Black Categories' who were denied state-allotted jobs. In the end, missing out on the piece of curtain was the least of his troubles. While the 'hardboard mansions' were being dismantled, the entrepreneur took advantage of the general chaos and stole a section of hardboard and two planks of wood to make furniture with later on. Someone saw him and reported him to the police. He was taken to the public security bureau and interrogated for hours. He was just fourteen at the time.

As night fell, the municipal Party secretary took on a magical air. The entrepreneur felt a sense of pride as he gazed at the line of dead bodies. At last he could enjoy the kind of authority that everyone deserves in life. The dead lay below him, eyes agape, mere witnesses to their own humiliation.

After the entrepreneur saw the play *The Ninth-Grade Sesame Seed Officer* about the altruistic Communist cadre, he was moved to act with a keener sense of social justice. He sent proletarians into the incinerator without exploiting them once. He didn't even check their teeth. (A gold tooth is worth an average family's yearly income in this town.) It was a case of 'Levelling out the rich and poor' or 'The sun shines after the rain'. That was how he saw it, anyway. As his own father's death was still fresh in his mind, he was always especially kind to rightists, or to anyone who had been run over by a car.

When he walked through the streets and saw people queuing up for the bus or stopping for a chat, scenes from the crematorium would flash through his mind: the oily vapours rising from charred skin, the slowly contracting skeletons. He would think about the difference between the yellow and orange skin of the roast chicken on the street stalls, and the tender white skin of a little girl's face before it enters the furnace. He would think about the difference between the living, who could move and talk, and the dead, who could neither move nor make excuses for themselves any longer.

His love for the dead grew deeper every day. He thought about how happy he would be if his mother were to become a dead person (that mouth shut once and for all). The dead had made him a millionaire, the leader of the crematorium's unofficial Party committee. The dead never talked nonsense. They never vetted his publications or checked his account books. They didn't care what he wore, where he lived or where he travelled to. As the number of corpses rose, their ages and personalities became increasingly varied, and his love for them grew stronger. Although the frequent power cuts led to corpse pile-ups (a chemical plant leaked once, flooding local fields with polluted water, seven people died in one day, and they were all brought to his shack at the same time, of course), he still felt that there were far too many living people and not enough dead.

As time went by, he became confused as to why people

insisted on living so long. When his mother swore at him for tearing off a button from what had been a perfect pair of woollen trousers (in fact it already had three buttons missing, and you could only find replacements for those foreign-style brass-effect buttons in decadent boom towns like Shenzhen), he suddenly imagined how calm she would look when she was dead. He imagined it again when he gazed at her through the sheet of red cotton they hung between each other before going to sleep. 'The Buddha's realm is full of mercy,' he wanted to tell her. He opened his mouth, but the words would not come out.

'Women burn better than men,' he told her again, but this time in a more insistent tone. 'Dead people smell like roast meat, when they first go in the oven.' A few minutes later, the innards let off foul gases that make you want to retch, but he kept that last part to himself.

'You should come to the shack one day and take a look,' he continued. 'There's an upholstered armchair that belonged to a rich and powerful man before the campaign against the "Four Olds". You can sit in it and watch the corpses entering the furnace and see them being transported by the music of their choice to a realm of peace and joy.'

'They say that one day, balls of cotton will fall from the sky,' the mother murmured, her shadow stretching along the pink wall behind her. 'When I see them fall, I will go with you to the shack.'

The son panicked. When he was young, his mother could always see through his lies. He was now in his thirties, but he still felt unsure of himself. 'Just come with me and have a look,' he said. 'That's all I'm asking.'

Just before daybreak, the mother glanced outside through the gaps in their wooden door. Then she turned her head, her green eyes glistening like the eyes of an old cat. The son dared not meet her gaze, but he could sense the importance of the moment. He knew there was something he had to do. He rolled over and got out of bed.

The mother and son seemed troubled by the way the day had begun. The routine of their mornings had been upset. Usually, when the son pulled back the red curtain, the mother would press down the handle to open the front door. While the mother fed charcoal briquettes into the stove, the son would cross the smoke-filled room with a toothbrush in his mouth and step outside into the entrance passage to clean his teeth. After the mother had placed her chamber pot on the other side of the stove, the son would walk in, put down his toothbrush, pick up the chamber pot and carry it to the public latrines. Today, however, everything was out of sequence. It was so bad that, when he was squeezing out the toothpaste, his mother was squatting on the chamber pot for a piss. He was only supposed to hear her do that first thing in the morning, while he was still half asleep in bed.

It seemed like the start of something new. He realised it was time for him to act, but he didn't know where to begin.

Over the previous two years, he had made a life for himself. His business had succeeded beyond his wildest expectations. He had bought the electric kiln because he liked it, it intrigued him. He only discovered it could be used for burning bodies in a conversation he overheard in the public latrines. He set up his crematorium, and soon the bodies were churning out from the furnace like water from a pump, and he was continually rushing back and forth like the water pump's revolving chain, because in this town, rain or shine, whether it was a Sunday afternoon or a Wednesday night, people died every day. Sunday was never a day of rest, in fact people died more than ever. Especially women – women always chose to kill themselves on Sundays. Students between the ages of sixteen and twenty preferred to die on Mondays. Middle-aged housewives died on Tuesdays. This was the worst day for the entrepreneur, as he had to lug those huge fat women about the room all by himself. Babies and women who died in childbirth turned up on Wednesdays and Thursdays. Senior Party cadres died on Fridays. This was always a solemn and nerve-racking day. He would have to analyse the newspaper obituaries in minute detail to determine whether the deceased was a reformist or a reactionary, and then make the appropriate preparations for their swoon. People in their twenties liked to die on Saturday nights. Some would die on their way to a date, others in the drunken stupor after a break-up. Saturday was always the most romantic night of the week. Love would surge into the crematorium like fresh blood, and the cassette player on the rickety table would belt out Orff's 'Fortune, Empress of the World' all through the night.

The son watched his mother's shadow slip down the wall, creep across the grey cement floor and slowly disappear into the coal stove.

The morning passed quietly.

In the afternoon, the mother carefully combed her hair into place and followed her son outside. She locked the front door behind her, sat down on the back of her son's motorbike and, for the first time in seventeen years, left home. (A street writer from another province who wrote letters for the illiterate moved into the shed a few weeks later.) Then she left the town. She had never travelled further than five blocks from her home in her entire life.

She already looked like a swooner. She was dressed head to toe in burial clothes that had been worn by many swooners before her. On her way to the crematorium, everyone stopped and stared at the living woman dressed in dead men's clothes. She was even wearing ceremonial paper ingot shoes on her feet. Some recognised her as the old woman who lived in the Swooners' liaison office. As they reached the outskirts of the town the sun came out. The sky was blue, and there was not one cotton ball in the air.

The son led his mother inside the shack and stared at her. He saw now that she was a swooner like any other, and no longer had control over him. In fact, their roles seemed to have reversed. Were he to have called this woman his 'mother', his scalp would have split apart. She had nothing to do with him now. In the cool of the shack, he suddenly felt sure of himself and comfortable in the role he was about to take on. He was capable of change after all. Before today, he had always been playing a part that had been assigned to him, he'd had no choice in the matter. He was only ever his mother's son, the Party's son, the Motherland's son. He was a son right down to his bones, always taking the supporting role. But now, as he stared at the swooner standing before him, he finally sensed that he was separate from her, an individual, although he was not sure who that individual was yet. All he knew was that he wasn't a wily businessman, a smug clandestine leader, or the son of the dead rightist, the boy his schoolmates liked to kick about.

(It's very hard to draw the line between man and beast, the professional writer thinks to himself. What should the criteria be? A wolf will die to save her cubs, but a man will sell his mother for eight hundred yuan. A tiger will maim a weaker animal in its fight for food, but a man will go hungry until he's sure that his family's stomachs are full. You can't draw any conclusions from this . . .)

His entire life had been bound up with his mother and the experiences he had shared with her. He had worked like a dog to keep them both alive, because if they were going to survive in this world, they would have to pay rent, water bills, gas bills, buy vast quantities of compulsory premium bonds and cope with the inflation brought about by the Open Door Policy. When he bought the art school's electric furnace, he had no idea what the future had in store for him, or what talents he would prove to have. Now that he thought about it, he guessed that he had inherited his artistic sensibility from his mother. When he was a child, the old cabbage face would jump around the room like a monkey, humming 'When Will My Prince Come Back?' She knew all the popular songs from the 1930s, and passed on her love of music to her son. (That rightist had married her for her voice, and when he was run over on the street, his mind was filled with happy memories.) Although the son could no longer detect any traces of her past charms, he knew that the ordinary-looking woman in front of him was the only living woman he'd had any contact with. It was she who had brought him up. This thought was particularly repugnant to him when he heard the piss fall from between her legs in the morning, and caught the smell of her warm urine. He had thought he could never escape the lifetime sentence of being a 'son', but just when he was about to give up hope, fate showed him a light.

Now at last this heavy old swooner's body, which had consumed two deep-fried buns and a bowl of bean curd for breakfast, was finally going to join the ranks of the dead. He knew what remained to be done, but the suddenness of the events had knocked him sideways. He was no longer the cock-sure underground Party secretary. He could tell this was real, he could even smell his own body odours on his mother's skin. But there was a strange sense of theatre about the old woman dressed in burial clothes. His mother seemed at ease with the situation though; she thought she was in control, just as she had been in the office. She appeared to be watching her son's movements with a remote control in her hand.

He observed her scuttling between the corpses like a cock-roach, checking their hands and teeth, criticising their dress sense.

'This woman's still got her bracelet on,' she said, kneeling down.

The son walked over, lifted the dead woman's hand, inspected the bracelet and tugged it off her wrist.

'I know this man. He worked in the pharmacy on Peace Road.' The mother's paper ingot shoes brushed against another cadaver's head. She seemed excited. The son switched on the furnace briefly to check that the electricity was running.

'Burn him first,' she said, checking the pharmacist's hands and teeth. 'He knew I like dry turnips, the ones I soak and use to stuff dumplings with.'

The pharmacist was pushed into the furnace to the strains of 'The Internationale'. (After his death, he had been granted post-humous membership of the Chinese Communist Party.) When the son had locked the steel door, the mother switched on the furnace again, and her eyes sparkled like a young girl full of dreams and curiosity. Before she had married the art teacher who was later condemned as a rightist, she had laughed when her grandmother announced that her father had just hurled himself from the top of a building. At the time, she ignored her grandmother's tears, and instead remembered how the leader of the Central Committee had described the Shanghai capitalists who jumped off the top of tall buildings for fear of Communist persecution as 'parachuters'. She thought it was a very funny and accurate description.

'You monster,' the grandmother shouted, and slapped her innocent little face. 'Your father falls down and cracks his skull open and you just laugh about it.'

Her grandmother's eyes flashed with anger, but all she could do was giggle. She had no idea yet what death was. But soon after she married the rightist, she realised that these calamities can happen, and that she would have to spend the rest of her days using all her skill and cunning just to try to stay alive. She never liked to dwell on her past, though. As long as she was kept fed, she thought she could muddle her way through this cruel world, unless one day she decided to bring her life to an end, of course. She accepted that hardship and suffering were inevitable. Besides, if life became too easy, the skills she had developed over the years would be of no use to her any longer, and there would be nothing left for her to do but die. If, however, it turned out that death was not a tragedy, but a new way of life, an escape, then it might begin to look quite attractive to her.

She sat in the armchair, combing her shiny black hair, waiting for the posthumous Party member to emerge from the oven. She wondered whether she would take her gold earrings in with her or not, when her time came.

The son pulled out the metal tray.

The pharmacist was immaculately white. He looked like he had just come out of a shower. A soft fragrance rose from his tidy white bones. The flesh had disappeared from his body. The mother was relieved to see that his horrible fat lips had disappeared too.

'He is utterly transformed,' she said, pressing the hot white bones with delight.

'They're nice and soft, aren't they?' Now his flesh had gone, the pharmacist had become ageless. Had one not seen him go into the oven, one might have taken him for a child, or a creature from some heavenly realm.

'My god!' the mother cried, beating her chest. 'If only I had known before.'

The son could guess what his mother meant by these words. He presumed that she was contemplating 'immortality' – that word he heard so often at funeral receptions. She knew now that the posthumous Party member had achieved immortality.

'He is immortal now,' the son said. 'Whether he goes to heaven or hell, he won't be coming back here again. Especially considering he managed to get through life without committing any grave mistakes.' He walked to the cassette player and turned off 'The Internationale', then put on an aria from *Salammbô* free of charge.

The joy of seeing the pharmacist shed his mortal coil put the mother and son in convivial mood. They moved their hands inside the pharmacist's hot carcass and soaked up the mysterious wonder of death. The son noticed with embarrassment a scrap of steaming flesh stuck to the furnace door – a clumsy slip-up on his part – and quickly unhooked it with a metal rod.

'What music did you play just then?' the mother asked in a melodious tone.

'Mussorgsky's *Salammbô*,' the son replied.

'Musso - who?' The mother obviously knew nothing about modern music.

'It's probably a little contemporary for your taste.' The son was unwilling to give detailed responses to uninformed questions.

'I wouldn't mind using that piece for myself.'

The son paused for a moment, and whispered, 'I still have the old recording of you singing the . . . dirty songs.'

'All right. But start me off with the *Salammbô*.'

'It doesn't matter what music I play, you will still come out of the oven as white as snow.'

'Immaculate? Do you promise?' The mother sounded as though she were talking to a wily tradesman.

'Immaculate, as long as there's no power cut.' Then he added, out of a sense of professional duty: 'Sometimes middle-aged women come out slightly yellow, a pale yellow like golden corn. But I'll do my best to make you come out even whiter than the pharmacist.'

With this new feeling of trust established between them, their eyes could at last meet. They had reached a silent understanding. They felt even closer now than when they had witnessed the pharmacist's transformation. Before, the son had always thought of his mother as a grandmother wolf. As a child, he was terrified that when she tied a scarf around her head, her white ears would suddenly pop out. When he heard her hum he wanted to run away; he was frightened that as soon as she was happy, her grey tail would stick out from under her skirt and wag from side to side. But now that they were looking into each other's eyes for probably the first time in their lives, they felt more united than the day he was interrogated in the public security bureau and their entire future was at stake.

'As long as there's no power cut,' the son pledged, 'I will give you a beautiful burn.' He was getting excited now. He turned round, and with a piece of bent wire, plucked out from a crack in the table an original Hong Kong tape of Deng Lijun's songs. It was the tape that Premier Deng Xiaoping had specifically banned, the one with the dirty song 'When Will My Prince Come Back?' The song had the decadent chorus his mother used to sing: 'Come drive away the loneliness from my love-sick heart . . .'

The son was raring to go. He put his past resentments towards his mother behind him, and devoted himself to her needs. They no longer behaved as they had done in the shed in the entrance passage, grunting cursory replies to each other's questions, glancing at one another with contempt. They were now united in one action, bound together as intimately as a pair of identical twins. They breathed a sigh of relief. This quiet understanding was as comforting as the soft and warm white bones. The mother's face glowed with maternal love. She was a woman who had sung dirty songs in her youth, and whose eyes had sent a painter crazy. In the old woman's face, these eyes now looked gentle and kind. That expression has disappeared from today's world. You can walk the streets for ten years and never find an expression like it. (At least you won't find it on Chinese faces. Perhaps Western faces can look gentle, calm, kind. But in China, not only have those expressions disappeared, but so have all similar expressions of pity, compassion and respect.)

Anyone observing the couple through the window could have only guessed at the intense feelings welling up inside them. The shameful idea that had come to the entrepreneur the night before had now transformed into a glorious mission. He fetched the box with the pharmacist's photograph on the lid, tipped some of the ashes into it, opened the window, tossed out the remaining ashes, and closed the window again. (One day he forgot to shut the window, and the stray dogs loitering outside sneaked in and gobbled up half of the twelve swooners that were lying on the floor.) He washed down the hot metal tray with a wet flannel, and dropped the tape into the cassette player. Everything was in order, everything had gone according to plan. All that was left to be done was for the mother to lie down on the tray. 'It's ready now,' he said to her softly.

She lay down flat on the tray, just as she had seen the post-humous Party member do. She let her hands drop naturally to the sides and fixed her eyes on the ceiling. As the son was about to switch the furnace on, the mother raised her hand in the air and said, 'Play the music!'

'All right,' he said. He leaned back and pressed the play button, waited for the prelude to finish, then slowly pushed the tray into the furnace to the rhythm of the *Salammbô* aria. The paper ingot shoes were the last to go in. Stuck to the soles he saw a patch of grey ash and a brightly shining drawing pin.

'The electricity bill's under the premium bonds!' he heard his mother cry from inside the furnace, as the lyrics of the dirty song began to blare out. Without a word, he brushed his hair back and slammed the steel door shut.

The Suicide *or* The Actress

Su Yun was sixteen when she first stepped onto the stage. It was the height of the Cultural Revolution, and she was determined to pour all her youth and vitality into the revolutionary heroines she played. She took the roles of Jiang Jie, the brave activist who is shot in a Guomindang jail, and Liu Hulan, the Communist martyr who is decapitated by Japanese invaders. She sang the part of the shepherdess who loses her feet to frostbite in her attempt to rescue her state-owned flock, and danced the role of the fearless peasant leader, Wu Jinghua, who bayonets the evil capitalist landowner.

But the winds brought in by the Open Door Policy blew away those revolutionary heroines, and Su Yun lost her way. She tried to keep up with the changing times and relax her moral views, but was kicked back time and again by a series of failed love affairs. She slowly lost her grip on reality and retreated inside herself. She wanted to travel to the core of her being, to see what lay at her life's end.

Su Yun's initial plan was to die alone, but she was afraid that without an audience, her performance would go unnoticed. When she thought that she would soon become a heap of white powder inside a blazing incinerator, her heart clenched.

What if she shed no tears at the moment of death? She was incapable of predicting how she would react. When she tried to imagine taking her last breath, crazed thoughts fluttered through her mind like dry petals falling from a withered bunch of flowers. A laugh rose from the pit of her stomach.

Her life seemed like the string of maxims she copied from magazines, then tore up and tossed on the floor. These maxims gave her strength and insight. They taught her, for example, that 'a sage must assume the guise of a fool'. As well as jotting down these maxims, she also liked to copy out from Milan Kundera's books passages that mock female frailty. 'He really must hate women,' she said to herself. 'He implies that without us, the world would be a better place. What a cheek! Although, I must admit, my foolish behaviour today does seem to support his argument.'

She felt as though she had lived a hundred years. Everything that happened in the world seemed to her like a tedious repetition of some past event. One day she made up her mind to write a play about a woman who wants to commit suicide. She tried to remain objective, but couldn't help writing herself into the script. While she worked on her suicide play, she continued her career as an actress, having to die day after day on stage. The strain was almost too much for her to bear. In the midst of her distress, a new idea came to her. She decided that in her play she would return from death to perform her suicide once again.

As her thoughts took shape, she sat down at her desk and set to work on her second draft. First she sketched an outline of the male lead, who was a composite of her current boyfriend – a painter who worked in the municipal museum – and several other men she had known.

She made the lead a little taller and bulkier than her boyfriend, and gave him a graveyard voice that suggested a sentimental character and a long history of heartbreak. Through his untidy, tobacco-stained teeth, she made him spew a few of the vulgar terms and phrases that filled the latest magazines – words like: IQ, spiritual enlightenment, 'my bleeding heart', 'too vile for words', and 'chasing skirt'. This was her idea of the perfect man.

In real life this man was cold and arrogant, and showed her little respect. But in her play, he became her servant – the meat under her knife that she could dissect and analyse as she pleased.

Having assigned him his correct position, she smiled to herself and lowered her pen. She knew that in dealings with people, it is essential to first assign positions. This applied not only to her

44

and to him, but to the four billion other people on this planet. No human contact is possible without first assigning positions. If two people are talking to each without prior knowledge of their respective ranks, they will achieve nothing. They might as well be talking to themselves.

Before she lifted her pen again, she flicked through her notebook and read a couple of remarks she had jotted down about him:

> He is lying in bed moaning about how tired he is. It's all an act. He just wants me to go over to him so that he can pull me down and have his way with me. He didn't ejaculate last night when we made love, so he is desperate for my body.

> I have noticed that since the three-legged dog moved in with him, he has been less attentive to me, and his outlook on life seems to have matured.

She felt distanced from these remarks. Reading them now, they seemed to her like the vague and shadowy dreams that drift away upon waking from a deep sleep. She found it hard to separate the stories she had written from the events in her real life. But already she saw herself as the lead actress in her play, and the only member of her audience.

Gradually, she felt that her life was being taken over by her character in the play, or that she had somehow become that character in real life – a failure of a woman who had the impertinence to tell others how to lead their lives. Her different selves suffered from different afflictions, making it impossible for her to know where she stood in relation to others. She longed to escape and free herself from her troubled existence. She tried taking an overdose of sleeping pills, but didn't manage to lose consciousness. Later, she consulted the works of Heidegger, hoping to use his philosophy to untangle the mess in her mind, but after wading through a couple of tomes she discovered that Heidegger was even more confused than she was.

Realising there was no other choice left for her, she made up her mind once and for all to take her life during a suicide attempt.

'If only everyone could get on with each other!' she cried.

She wanted to go and talk to the painter, the man she both loved and pitied. But ever since he started looking after the three-legged dog, he seemed to have lost interest in her. All she could do now was write her play, incorporate him into the narrative (whether he liked it or not), then kill herself for him, to fill the emptiness in her soul.

Her play embarrassed her. She was afraid of looking back over what she had written because she knew there was little difference between her life and her script. Looking back would have been tantamount to returning to her past. The self in the script was tainted with all her own traits and experiences. She grew accustomed to calling the woman in her script 'I'.

As the weeks passed, she felt like an old bunch of grapes that was fermenting in the sticky mess of life, waiting to distil into a pure and transparent wine, then evaporate into thin air.

'The vagina is a very depraved dance-floor,' she scribbled in her notebook.

Her thoughts drifted back over the last decade. The painter was probably her longest-staying partner on this dance-floor. The other men who turned up occasionally, including the professional writer, the blood donor and a friend from drama college, only stayed long enough to dance a tango or a jig before retreating into the background. Although she was unwilling to include these minor characters into her play, she couldn't wipe them from her memory, and in the end they somehow or other managed to find their way onto the page. As she constantly oscillated between her script and her life, her mind became confused and feverish.

When she was not working on her play, the emptiness that engulfed her at dawn, at midday, and especially on summer afternoons, dragged her spirits down. She suspected that her writing was merely an excuse to waste time. 'Everything I bring to completion is dull and meaningless,' she wrote to herself several times.

But she needed to keep writing. Although she knew she had little control over her actions, she sensed she was somehow participating in them. She suspected that the professional writer was secretly writing about her, and this increased her unease.

'It's God's fault. He is the cause of all this trouble,' she cried out from her script. 'Why does He punish me in this way? First I lived within His lies, then I lived within my own. Now I'm not sure whether all of this is just a lie too. I have to assume that everyone feels this way. You ask me why I lie. Well I could ask you, "Why should I not lie?" Have you not heard any of His lies yet?'

Once she had calmed down a little, she lowered her head and thought for a while, then started to plan the stage design for her play.

'The backdrop of the stage is a single piece of hardboard,' she wrote in her notebook. 'If there is a clock in the props department, hang it up. If not, paint one, but make sure to attach metal dials to it. When the clock strikes the hour, the stagehands must rush behind the hardboard and turn the dials to eleven. (A mark should be painted behind the clock to show them how far to turn.)

'Dress: The female lead should wear one of the chiffon nightgowns criticised in the latest Open Door Policy memorandum. If the club's Party secretary permits, the top three buttons can be left undone and the sleeves rolled up a little. Deal with this matter in accordance with current levels of reform. The chairs should date from before the campaign against the "Four Olds". The Party secretary must understand that the female lead is corrupted by the evils of Bourgeois Liberalisation, and is not fit to sit on a revolutionary-style chair. The table in the corner of the room can be fake.'

From the piles of paper on her desk, she picked up a few pages of script and started reading them aloud. It was a scene in which her alter ego, Su Su, is visited by Li Liao and Old Xing – two characters based respectively on the professional writer and the blood donor.

A small single room in the actors' quarters above the Jiefang District art centre.

LI LIAO: [*Knocks on the door.*] Su Su! [*Knocks again.*] It's me! [*SU SU gets up slowly from her chair and walks towards the door.*] I waited two hours for you in the restaurant. I thought something must have happened to you.
[*LI LIAO walks in and stands beside SU SU's chair. His lined face resembles a walnut. SU SU averts her gaze and links her hands across her chest.*]

LI LIAO: What's the matter? [*He notices the awkward expression on her face.*]

SU SU: Old Xing's just been round.

LI LIAO: So?

SU SU: I said yes to him. I said I would marry him.
[*The actor playing LI LIAO can improvise on his expression here, but should not resort to knocking the chair over.*]

LI LIAO: We've been seeing each other for nearly a year now, and we've never had a row. Why would you want to marry him?

SU SU: The fact is, I don't love you.

LI LIAO: But you told me you loved me.

SU SU: So what? Why do you believe everything I say? Didn't you say yourself that women are incapable of telling the truth?

LI LIAO: I have grown used to the way your words differ from your actions. In fact, I'm starting to find it quite sweet.

SU SU: I'm sorry, women are made of salt, not sugar . . .

Su Yun carried the pages to her bed and lay down. In the rehearsal room below, the art centre's orchestra was tuning up. She lit a cigarette with one hand and continued reading the script.

48

LI LIAO: How can you marry him? Do you really think he's
             better than me? When he stands up straight, he
             doesn't even reach your shoulders. Is it because
             he's got money, and his pockets are stuffed with
             Foreign Exchange Certificates and egg ration
             tickets? Or are you playing one of your little
             games? Is this just another act?

The orchestra below swelled in a sudden crescendo. It sounded
like an earthquake. Above the roar, a soprano belted out
flirtatiously: '*The girls are as pretty as flowers. How the men love to
gaze upon them!* . . .'
    Su Yun could no longer hear herself speak. She repeated: 'Is
this just another act?' at the top of her voice, but the words were
drowned by the music.
    She listened to the French horns and trombones struggling to
play in unison. The drums were so loud they made the
floorboards shake and the old lamp on her desk flicker. She
noticed an eye of the white cat in the framed picture on her wall
turn from blue to red.

LI LIAO: What did I do wrong?
SU SU: Don't ask, don't ask. [*She is almost shouting now, but
             her expression is still calm.*] We should call it a day.
             I stopped loving you ages ago. I only said I loved
             you when I was caught in the heat of the moment.
             It didn't count.
LI LIAO: Does what you say now count?
SU SU: Yes.
LI LIAO: I don't believe you! I've heard you say all this a
             hundred times before.
             [*They glare ferociously at one another. SU SU's fierce
             expression is out of keeping with her flowery nightgown.
             The stagehands should prepare to turn the dials to eleven
             when the clock strikes the hour.*]
SU SU: It's getting late, you should be on your way.
             [*Just as LI LIAO is about to storm off stage, OLD*

49

XING walks through the door. This man is short and deathly pale. He is dressed in a Western suit and platform heels. Standing next to him, LI LIAO looks like a tramp in his tattered shirt and scruffy plimsolls. OLD XING leans down, pulls out a present from his bag and, with both hands, offers it to SU SU.]

OLD XING: This is for you. It's a pack of imported cigarettes.

SU SU: Thank you. Don't bother taking your shoes off. Come in, come in!

'Our glorious Motherland. The place I grew up. On this infinite expanse of . . .' As the soprano paused for breath, Su Yun shouted out again: 'Come in, come in!' The soprano belted out a final *'Aaaah'* as the drums rolled into a frenetic climax, then suddenly a magical calm descended upon the room – a calm similar to the relief one feels after revealing one's naked body to another person for the first time. Su Yun lowered her voice to a whisper.

LI LIAO: So when did you accept his proposal?

SU SU: An hour ago.

LI LIAO: Well that's that then.

SU SU: I have the right to choose my own path in life.

LI LIAO: Yes, but you have no right to lie.

'This is not true,' Su Yun scribbled fiercely across her script, under the words 'I said I would marry him'.

In fact, she had never loved either of these two men. She had only got involved with them because she wanted to make the painter jealous and stir him from his apathy. But her acting skills were still quite rudimentary at the time, and she had little understanding of her role. In reality, all she wanted was a chance to flaunt her female charms and entwine men in her web of lies. In this world, lies are unavoidable, and are sometimes very useful. Men presume that women only cry when they are upset, but women know very well that their tears fall as easily as piss.

She wiped her tears dry, put her pen down and stared at herself in the mirror: a little taller than the average woman, a pair of big dark eyes that attracted the gaze of every passing man. As far as she was concerned, her beauty was only of use to men, it was a nuisance to herself (although she would have been upset if people had ceased to look at her). She knew that, from an early age, she had been forced to employ a large portion of her energies fending off the lecherous advances of her male admirers, and had consequently lost sight of the more important things she should have been doing with her life.

But writing the play gave her a sense of inner worth. As she continued to work on her script, the men in her life left her dance-floor and retreated to their seats in the corner. At last she was able to take the lead role and march forward with her head held high. She trod on air. Now, each man she encountered seemed as dull as wax. The triumphant expression on their faces after they had slept with her filled her with disgust. Love always ends in failure, she told herself at the end of each affair.

'Who do you think you are? You wretch!' she scribbled to herself in the margins of her script.

One night, on the back of her script she wrote a letter to the painter:

My sweetheart, the time has come for us to part. Will you ever know how much I loved you? Life is an illusion, only you are real. The one thing my suicide will prove is that I am a failure, and that I have nothing to my name. When I was with you, my hands were filled with petals of love. Without thinking, I tossed them in the air and the wind carried them away.

The characters in her play and in her life exhausted her. She tried to guess what the professional writer who was composing a story about her had planned for her future. She tried to guess what she herself had planned for her future, and who would end up killing whom. This state of being calm on the outside but restless within put her in mind of two actors she had seen swimming across the television screen dressed in heavy octopus costumes. She could sense the pain it had caused them to move so slowly and seemingly at ease. She was now living in the calm that heralds the approach of middle age. She knew that time was running out, and wished that she or the writer would quickly bring her story to an end and consign her to oblivion.

But as soon as she attached herself to her character in the play, her spirits lifted a little. She didn't realise that writing is a meaningless act of vanity, and that she was merely patching a few people and events together in order make her life seem more interesting. She took the lead role of her play, and through her eyes, she was able see how stupid and naïve men are. She wondered how these poor souls could ever hope to find a 'graceful companion' among a generation of women who had grown up reading *Analysis of the Dictatorship of the Proletariat* and *The Fall of Chiang Kaishek*. Today's women are corrupted. How can you expect a girl who has grown up reading *Selected Writings of Mao Zedong* to be cultivated, elegant or refined?

'Men force us to wear these fripperies,' she wrote to herself. 'When they fall in love, they give us jewellery, dress us up, and allow us to twist them around our little fingers. They never see the vulgar thoughts that lie hidden beneath our smiles. All my tastes and ideas are formed for their benefit. They fall in love with the woman they have created from us.'

She remembered the wolf-man featured in a television documentary. A few days after she had seen the programme, the wolf-man appeared to her again, popping up between a man and woman who were locked in an embrace. Later, she saw it peering furtively from between two brick houses, from under the brim of a little girl's hat, from inside a bus and from behind the glass pane of a shop window. The wolf-man could only stand on all fours. She was always terrified it might appear one day between the lines of her script.

Slowly it dawned on her that her character was planning something, something she would only find out about after the event had taken place. In her script, she placed herself in situations she would never have experienced in real life (although later she realised that these situations were in fact variations of events in her past). In this way she was able to detach her spirit from her body and place it in a position from which she could learn new things about herself and discover how others behaved towards her. She was like the wolf-man, crouching in a dark corner, staring at herself.

First she realised that the innocence she had projected in the past was a sham. She discovered that she was constantly scheming, and that when she was swooning in the smell of fresh flowers and the sight of blue skies, she always had one eye firmly open. Even when she was immersed in her writing, she never managed to close that eye. In her play she slowly revealed the ugliness a woman prefers to keep hidden: the bad breath that lurks behind her tidy white teeth; the lock of hair that appears to be falling casually over her face but is in fact deliberately concealing a wide chin; the silence she adopts to mask her ignorance; the loose clothes she wears to hide her flat chest. As she revealed these secrets, Su Yun suddenly caught sight of a ball of light, the mysterious glow that shines after a suicide attempt.

When the first scene of the second act was completed, she was confident she could finish the play, and began to look more closely at herself. First she analysed her reactions to men's gestures, body heat, sticky fluids, and the sounds and smells that issue from their internal organs. She remembered the first time she saw a man's dark and dirty testicles, and the wrinkled stump that dangles between. Then she remembered how this man had pressed down upon her, and how the hole whose use she had been unaware of until then was suddenly filled with his hideously gyrating flesh. After she'd slept with him, she knew she would be incapable of feeling shy or innocent again. When she let the next man smear his sticky white mess across her thighs, she felt dirty and abused. She realised she was no longer a child, and that in order to appear like other women, she would have to walk outside with a smile on her face even though she felt as though she had been wiped down with an oily cloth. She understood that she would have to start pretending, and that this is what everyone did. Everyone has to learn to hide their feelings and get on with life.

As time passed, she grew accustomed to the slimy male fluids and the various ways men moved: stomping down the streets with their heads in the air, thrusting back and forth during intercourse, chomping noisily at their food at mealtimes. She learned about men's cruelty and weakness, and became familiar with the smell of their feet and dirty plimsolls, the stench of tobacco on their teeth.

'They invaded every part of me,' she wrote. 'They wanted my chastity, but they didn't respect it. I wanted their love, but they just pulled out their dicks and squirted their sperm over me. They destroyed all my dreams. Where can I hope to find love now? They have polluted all the sources. Just because they have stolen my innocence from me, does that mean I must lay myself bare and expose every part of myself to them? If I don't put on an act, how will I ever find love? Men are no better than dogs. They believe that when they lift their legs to piss, the ground beneath them becomes their territory. If I don't conceal my true nature, how can I satisfy their desire for feminine restraint and refinement?'

As she progressed with her suicide plan, she caught a glimpse of her future, and she felt both calm and afraid. She was nervous that someone might guess her state of mind, so before she stepped outside, she always made sure to dress up like a woman who was passionately in love with life. 'All suffering is man-made,' she said, trying to console herself. 'The sublime state of confusion is only possible when your heart is numb. Suicide is the only permanent cure for despair.' She forbade herself from thinking about her birth or her death. She knew that her birth and death were travelling in different directions, but heading for the same goal.

When she decided that suicide was the natural way to finish the play, she tore up the earlier scenes she had been working on and started again from scratch. She hoped that the new one-act play she came up with would bring her life to a glorious and radiant end. She dedicated the new script to the love she had once believed in, hoping that this would soothe her broken heart. She telephoned the Open Door Club, a venue filled with the type of liberal-minded people who had appeared since the launch of the reform policy. She wanted to use this club to stage the final climax of her life.

In the centre of the newly built club was a large basketball court. The space below the spectators' seats was occupied by ping-pong rooms, rehearsal rooms, shops, the offices of an association for the handicapped, a social club for retired cadres, a local family planning centre, a senior citizens' dating agency, a wholesale outlet for Victory Biscuits, and a tax-collection point. Walking through the club, one would bump into unemployed youths, company managers, artists, the two midgets who danced with the club's singer every night, painters on the look-out for beautiful models, and women in search of their prince on a white horse.

A few months before, the club had hosted the first beauty contest to take place in the town since the launch of the Open Door Policy. When the young women glided across the stage, a beautiful scent flowed from their thighs, nipples, stomach, feet, backs and buttocks, and filled the competition hall. The first part of the contest was a quiz on the memorandums issued at the Ninth Party Conference. The eventual winner had spent six months studying the documents, and got every question right. The last test was the swimwear competition. The women waltzed delicately across the stage, as the choir behind them sang: '*Let us follow the advice of the Party Central Committee, and go to the rivers, lakes and seas to perform our morning exercises . . .*'

Inside the club, people could gain a taste of what it feels like to travel abroad. They would swagger through the corridors, exchanging looks of smug satisfaction. The shops below the spectators' seats had American cigarettes and bars of soap whose wrappers were printed with pictures of foreign women in their underwear. The soap wasn't for sale, it was merely displayed to bring in the customers. Young men would enter the shop pretending to want to buy something, just so they could lean over the glass counter and stare at the smooth shoulders of the lady with golden hair, then with palpitating hearts, lower their gaze to her ample breasts and the flesh-coloured bra that covered them. With each new campaign against 'Bourgeois

Liberalisation', the soap wrapper was assessed by censors from the Information Bureau and Propaganda Bureau, but always managed to pass the test. You could say that the wrapper lay on the boundary between the pornographic and the healthy.

In the club's video rooms and coffee bars, members swapped Foreign Exchange Certificates and ration coupons. The club became the centre of the town's black market trade. One could find coupons for peanut oil, as well as the diesel coupons and national treasury bonds that were introduced after the launch of the Open Door Policy. Two tickets for the monthly screening of films marked 'Internal Viewing Only' (which only a select group of cadres were allowed to 'Watch and Criticise') could be acquired in exchange for a permit to buy goods at the Friendship Store, which was generally reserved for foreign visitors. If one had recently embarked on a new love affair, two of these tickets would guarantee a night of passion. These films had not yet been vetted by the Central Committee, so it is easy to imagine the kind of scenes they contained. In the coffee bar, one could also exchange lithium batteries for Marlboro cigarettes, a bottle of foreign wine for a bicycle, a copy of *Lady Chatterley's Lover* for the second volume of the erotic classic, *Jin Ping Mei*, a hundred treasury bonds for a jar of Nescafe, and top grade rice coupons for an advertisement bearing the picture of a blonde woman in a swimsuit. One could also procure photocopies of the application forms and correspondence addresses of every large university in America, as well as a list of the names and telephone numbers of the staff of Beijing's American Embassy. These of course had to be paid for in Foreign Exchange Certificates, as indeed did anything with remotely 'foreign' associations. With a wad of FECs and a couple of purchasing permits, you could wander into the Friendship Store without being stopped by the guards. If you were lucky, you might even be able to rub shoulders with a foreigner inside the store, and catch a whiff of their intoxicating bourgeois fragrance.

Su Yun knew that the painter often visited the Open Door Club to watch the various talent and beauty contests that were held inside.

She made an appointment with the club's manager and turned up at his office at the time agreed. He was the son of a commanding officer of the old Red Army. Although he was in his forties and had a small, monkey-like chin, the continuously changing lines on his brow suggested he was at the forefront of the reform process. During the Cultural Revolution, he was sent to prison because his father had been a lackey of the treacherous marshal, Peng Dehuai. His wrists were left crippled by the handcuffs, and since his aunt was living abroad at the time, he was accused of being an undercover agent, and subjected to further torture. However, after the Open Door Policy was launched, foreign connections and pockets stuffed with FECs gave him the freedom to saunter in and out of the Friendship Store whenever he pleased. After the posthumous rehabilitation of his father, he used the compensation money to set up the club, and threw himself into his new career with enormous enthusiasm.

'I want to take part in your "Everyone is Happy" show,' Su Yun told him, lowering herself into her seat. 'I will perform the most innovative act this town has ever seen.'

'You're from the Jiefang District art centre, am I right?' the manager asked.

'The newspapers have reported that this act is very popular in Japan.'

The manager's affection for all things foreign had turned the hairs of his beard blond; his small blue-black eyes were a harmonious fusion of East and West. These eyes were now clearly drawn to Su Yun's larger-than-average breasts.

'My act will achieve record-breaking ticket sales for your club,' she stated calmly.

'I've seen you on stage,' the manager said, suddenly remembering her performance of the patriotic shepherdess.

'I don't expect any share of your profits. All I want is one free ticket.'

'What kind of act do you have in mind?' The manager wasn't interested in her answer, he just wanted an excuse to continue talking to her. In fact the acts for his 'Everyone is Happy' show had been finalised months before.

'What type of background music can you provide?' she asked.

'Even if your act is accepted by the censors, I'm afraid you'll have to wait until next year to perform it.'

'That won't do. I must perform it within the next three days,' she said, staring at the beady eyes behind his imported glasses.

'So what is this act then?' he asked.

'Suicide,' she said.

'Suicide?' The manager hadn't heard of this act before. He had to pause and think for a while. 'And it's the latest act from Japan, you say.'

'Yes, there have been articles about it in the magazines.'

'Is there real death involved, or is it just performance art?' the manager asked, removing his glasses.

'It's real suicide, in front of an audience.' After these words left her mouth, she was disappointed by how flat they sounded.

It was a hot day, and the downy hairs on Su Yun's shoulders were drowning in a thin layer of sweat. A fine rash had erupted on her skin, and her breasts felt awkward and heavy. Her slightly flabby stomach bulged through her tight white skirt like a lump of steamed rice. Sensing a sour dampness seep from her lower body, she crossed her legs, exposing her beautifully shaped calves.

'How could the audience watch you meet your death without wanting to rush onto the stage to rescue you?' he asked, breathing in the milky smells wafting from her body.

At last she had succeeded in letting her play precede her life. When she got home, she took out her notebook, and wrote down everything that was said during the meeting.

MANAGER: You will probably need to register first at the Suicide Prevention Centre.

SU SU: They all know me there already. Anyway, they're so overworked they are ready to commit suicide themselves!

MANAGER: Why not just pretend to kill yourself? You don't have to do it for real the first time.

SU SU: No one can tell the difference between what is real and fake any more. How else would I have got away with all my fake suicide attempts?

MANAGER: I spent four years in jail without ever once considering suicide.

SU SU: You're older than me. You lack a modern consciousness. Do you know that in foreign countries there are nudist beaches already?

[*The manager is dumb-struck by this astounding news from far-off lands. He stands up and walks from stage left to stage right. The volume of the background disco music gradually increases.*]

MANAGER: Which college did you attend?

SU SU: The teacher's college. I majored in politics.

MANAGER: That's one of the country's finest institutes of higher education. My son graduated from there too.

SU SU: It's not an institute of higher education – it's just a school where people are locked up and taught to know their place.

MANAGER: The teachers are excellent.

SU SU: It would be more accurate to call them prison officers.

MANAGER: Death is a terrifying thing.

SU SU: Mr Manager – I have seen bare wheatfields after the harvest.

[*She shakes her head emotively. Her passionate expression is in stark contrast to the beseeching demeanour she wore when she first entered the manager's office. She lights a cigarette, takes a deep drag and smiles dreamily as the smoke streams from her nostrils.*]

MANAGER: I'm afraid that I haven't yet received notification from the authorities that the term 'Mr' can be employed in the workplace.

SU SU: Didn't you hear Premier Deng use the term 'Mr Manager' at the state banquet? My death won't change a thing. The air will still be here for you to breathe. If you understood that you were a mere grain of dust in this life, you would know that suicide isn't a private matter – it needs an audience. That's the only reason I've come to see you today. If it were simply a matter of killing myself, I wouldn't need to go to so much trouble.

MANAGER: Have you just broken up with someone?

[*A light shines onto the backdrop, creating a sunset on the painted sky.*]

SU SU: I only came here to talk to you about the show. I should be on my way now, Mr Manager.

MANAGER: Can I invite you for a cup of coffee in the club?

SU SU: If it's to continue our discussion about the show.

MANAGER: Providing that you write out a will, and that your act promotes the message that socialist civilisation is on a forward march, then –

SU SU: You'll let me die right there on stage! Do you promise?

MANAGER: I'm still not entirely clear about your plans. What exactly will this act involve?

SU SU: I will hire a wild tiger from the zoo. It will chase me across the stage, I will run away from it, and in the end I will die between its jaws.

MANAGER: Aren't you afraid of tigers?

SU SU: I was born in the Year of the Tiger, but of course I'm as afraid of tigers as anyone else.

MANAGER: You're incredible! I will let you do it. I too was born in the Year of the Tiger.

SU SU: So you've lived twenty-four years longer than me.

At this point, the manager suddenly came to his senses. He stared at the 'dead' person sitting before him, and asked her: 'How much money do you want for this?'

'Nothing,' she replied. 'I will give my life away for free. If any part of my body happens to be of interest to you though, you're free to make use of it tonight. Tomorrow it will be good for nothing.'

The wrinkles on the manager's forehead suddenly smoothed out.

Three days later, a notice unlike any other that had appeared before was nailed to the entrance post of the Open Door Club.

TONIGHT OUR CLUB IS STAGING THE MOST GROUND-BREAKING SHOW IN THE WORLD: SUICIDE! IMPORTED FROM THE HIGHLY DEVELOPED NATION JAPAN, THE ACT IS BASED ON THE JAPANESE CONCEPT OF HARA-KIRI. THE PERFORMANCE WILL BANISH ALL SENSE OF SOLITUDE FROM THE SUICIDE VICTIM'S HEART. THERE IS NOW A WAITING LIST OF PEOPLE REQUESTING TO KILL THEMSELVES BEFORE AN AUDIENCE THAT RUNS UNTIL 1997. TONIGHT, THE ACTRESS IS COMRADE SU YUN. DESCENDED FROM A POOR PEASANT'S FAMILY, SHE IS A LEAGUE MEMBER, IN THE PRIME OF HER YOUTH — A STARTLINGLY BEAUTIFUL YOUNG WOMAN. IF YOU WOULD LIKE TO SEE THIS CHARMING LADY TAKE HER OWN LIFE, HURRY UP AND BUY A TICKET!
TICKET PRICE: 1 YUAN
TIME: 3 AM, JUNE 4TH

That night the club was engulfed by tens of thousands of hopeful spectators. Anyone who managed to buy tickets at the booth squeezed themselves into the crowd and sold the tickets on for ten times the price. Various impromptu street stalls sprang up on the margins of the crowd. One man selling nylon jackets held up a sign that read: IF YOU WANT TO SQUEEZE A PATH TO THE TICKET BOOTH, THESE NYLON JACKETS WILL EASE YOUR WAY, and the tracksuit tops on his fold-up table were sold in a matter of minutes. Soon customers who bought his nylon jackets could be seen swarming through the crowd like red cockroaches. Everyone squeezing out from the ticket booth emerged half their previous thickness. Five unfortunate ticket holders were dragged out from under the crowd's stamping feet. Four of them were already dead.

Su Yun hurriedly ran through the plot of the play in her mind as she stepped onto the stage in the basketball court. The audience exploded into rapturous applause, drowning the song 'Kill the Tiger and Climb the Hill' that was booming from the loudspeakers. The wild tiger entered the stage on its hind legs and waved at the audience; a team of athletes then strode confidently onto centre stage, and the audience continued to cheer and whistle. The tiger soon grew tired, and had to go back down on all fours, but it still managed to raise its front paw to the audience and wave cheerfully. Su Yun was wearing a clean white tracksuit. She had attached a plastic flower behind her right ear. Her skin looked rosy against her white clothes. She looked good enough to eat. Those in the know could tell from the blue piping that her tracksuit was imported and cost at least fifty FECs – domestically produced trousers didn't have that distinctive blue piping.

She glanced about her with a fixed smile on her face, trying to adopt the expression the Chinese women's volleyball team wore on their triumphant return from the Olympics. Unfortunately the tiger was looking the other way, and didn't see her confident grin. As the applause rose in a crescendo, Su Yun scanned the audience for the painter's face. She knew where he would be sitting. The day before, she had gone to see him at the municipal museum. She gave him a ticket, and told him it was for her one-woman show. When he asked her what act she was performing, she told him it was a suicide show. He smiled and said, 'That sounds very intriguing.' She searched the crowd once more, and at last caught sight of his panic-stricken eyes.

'He thinks I'm lying again,' she said to herself, 'or playing a game. When the tiger sinks its teeth into me though, he will feel sorry. But it will be too late. He will be upset to see my foot go, or my ear. That will bring him to his senses. The moment the tiger pounces on me, he'll scramble over the wire cage and come to my rescue.' She waved to him again, and he waved back. The noise of the crowd slowly died down. For a moment, she lost her will to perform, but her professional instincts took over. Twelve years of life as an actress enabled her to keep calm and move gracefully to centre stage.

She took a deep breath, then commenced the act she had decided upon in consultation with the club's manager. As the song 'The Peoples' Liberation Army and the People Go Together Like Fish and Water' started to play, she began a mime of washing the clothes of the beloved PLA soldiers. Half her mind was focused on the mime, the other half on the tiger. She knew that after she had hung the laundry out to dry, she would have to dance back to the army barracks, and the tiger – that 'class enemy' with the face of a man and the heart of a beast – would leap out from the bushes and dig its teeth into her. After she had died, the tiger would be caught and arrested. But on its way to the local police headquarters, a heroic PLA soldier would rush over to avenge her death by plunging a bayonet into the tiger's back. Marking the spot where Su Yun had been devoured, the soldiers would erect a heroine's plaque then sing 'The Internationale'.

As the plot raced through her mind, her steps became increasingly confused. Soon she looked like a Japanese puppet, bobbing up and down to the music's cheerful beat. Her gestures for rinsing the clothes were not in the least convincing. The script specified that she should now lift her skirt, dunk the clothes into a pail of fresh water and beat them with a stick as fiercely as the fictional hero Wu Song battled with the tiger in the famous episode from *Outlaws of the Marsh*. Unfortunately, the tiger before her misinterpreted her gestures as signs of aggression, and let out a horrific roar. She was aware she would have to improvise much of the action, because she hadn't had time to meet the tiger before the show, let alone conduct any rehearsals.

She skipped across the stage with tiny steps (which had once earned her the second prize in a local dance competition), moving closer and closer to the tiger. She gestured to it to circle her, but the tiger was panicked by her sudden movement and jumped three steps back. When the music blared out again, she took it as her cue to break into a song that expressed her joy at cleaning the clothes of the beloved Peoples' Liberation Army. She planted one foot in front of the other and wiggled her hips up and down. A fire exploded in her chest. 'Why is it taking so long?' she asked herself, determined not to look behind her to check what it was doing. 'Paper tiger!' she cursed. Then suddenly, without any warning, the tiger pounced forward, and well before it was planned for in the script, clamped its jaws around her chest.

The audience noticed two little horns sprout from the top of Su Yun's head, and watched her use them to try to fend the beast off. The people in the front rows could even hear her struggling to keep to her lines, squealing: '*The uniforms of our comrades, the PLA soldiers . . .*'

The tiger continued to lash out at her as she tried to prise from its jaws the uniform she was washing. Even the music that heralded the arrival of the beloved PLA soldiers did not deter the beast. The terms of the contract stipulated that the tiger was legally permitted to devour every part of her. The tiger attempted to clamp its jaws around her skull, but her two horns got in its way, so it decided to leave her head alone for the time being and start tucking into one of her arms. During this moment of respite, Su Yun craned her neck down through the space between the tiger's legs, and stared at the audience who were now howling with terror. The leg that wasn't crushed by the tiger's weight could still move freely. She lifted it in the air and gazed at the line of English words printed down the side of her tracksuit bottoms: WHEN YOU GO ABROAD, BE SURE TO WEAR WHITE! THEY SAY THAT THE STREETS IN FOREIGN COUNTRIES ARE AS CLEAN AS PUBLIC GARDENS. Very soon, only her horned head could move – every other part of her was crushed under the tiger's weight.

She met the tiger's gaze. Had the beast not smeared blood over her eyes, she would have been able to see very clearly the beautiful markings on its face, which were much more vivid than those on the toy tiger that hung on her wall (a birthday gift from an old boyfriend). The tiger stared at her eyes as it bit into her flesh. To her surprise, she quite enjoyed the sensation of being chewed; she had never experienced the feeling before. The audience screamed in horror. The tiger wiped its bloody mouth across her chest, then looked up and glanced at the commotion breaking out in the stalls. Su Yun took advantage of this pause to twist her head round and look in the painter's direction, but unfortunately her pathetic little horns obstructed her view.

Assuming that she was attempting to escape, the tiger dug its claws into her again and blocked the air from her nose and mouth. 'I love you, my darling,' she murmured to the painter. 'Now you know I wasn't lying. I want to start my life over again.'

She felt the tiger tuck into the area below her waist. Since she was unable to move, she hoped the tiger would first pull out her guts so as to cover up the parts that most attracted men's attention. She shook the animal's blood from her face, then lifted her head, hoping to catch a glimpse of the sky outside the window. The trembling horns on her head made her seem quite animated. Instead of the sky however, her eyes fell on the words of the red banner hanging from the chairman's podium: UPHOLD THE FOUR FUNDAMENTAL PRINCIPLES, CONSTRUCT SOCIALISM WITH CHINESE CHARACTERISTICS. Then, seated below the slogans, she saw the painter, utterly motionless, staring blankly at the stage.

'I love you,' she said to the tiger, without a hint of sarcasm. A second later, the remains of her dismembered body went stiff.

'May God have mercy on us,' the writer says. 'Every sin has its retribution.'

'We all receive our just deserts,' the blood donor adds. 'But I hope we get ours in this lifetime.'

'Were you in the audience when she committed suicide?' the writer asks, straightening his back.

'When who committed suicide?'

'That woman.' The writer can't bring himself to say her name. His square living room looks like a junk shop, with his belongings heaped along the walls. The furniture includes two chests, the revolving chair, plastic stool, a fold-up table donated by the Writers' Association, and a pair of armchairs. To give the room a neater appearance, he has pasted sheets of blank manuscript paper over the tears in the wallpaper left by the previous occupants. The only picture on the wall is a pencil sketch of a young girl that an ex-girlfriend of his gave him. Looking at it now, it strikes him that the picture is not as good as it once seemed. He thinks that if there were a woman in the room now, and a few more pieces of furniture, it might feel a little more comfortable. He leans over and puts a new tape into his cassette player. Verdi's *Requiem* fills the room, the soprano's voice soars to the ceiling. He slumps feebly back into his chair. 'That woman,' he repeats, turning the volume up a little.

The blood donor gets up and paces the room. Perhaps he has eaten too much. When he straightens his back he looks a little taller. 'Do you think you and I really understand each other?' he asks.

The writer glances at the blood donor and says: 'We understand each other better than we could ever understand a woman.' He leans over, turns the volume down again and sighs: 'A man whose heart has been wounded should take care in his relations with women.'

'It was stupid of me to propose to her.' The blood donor sucks on his cigarette then flicks the ash into a cup.

'I still don't understand why she went off with you,' the writer says. 'She and I were far more compatible. We shared the same interests and tastes. We even looked alike. But look at you – you're short and bald, you have no education, no manners . . .'

'It's history now. Put it behind you. We're friends aren't we? What do women matter? They just want a man to lean on, they don't mind who he is. Only friends care about a man's quality. Women are products of their environment. They want to pity the unfortunate and sponge off the rich. Together, we satisfied both these needs for her.'

'You mean to say you fulfilled her material needs and I fulfilled her spiritual ones,' the writer replies.

The blood donor crushes his cigarette out and lowers his head. 'What do you think drove her to it?' he asks.

'It amazes me that she managed to live so long. How did she survive all those years?' The writer then wipes the grease from his hands, and says to himself: We grew up in a spiritual vacuum, cut off from the rest of the world. A wasted generation. When the country started to open up, we were the first to fall. Foreign culture is the only religion now, but we have no means to understand it, or appreciate its worth. Half a century has gone by, and suddenly we find ourselves in the forest of modern life without a map or a compass. How can a society numbed by dictatorship ever find its way in the modern world? We are unable to think things through for ourselves, we have no reference points, we feel lost and out of our depth. We put on a show of superficial arrogance to hide our low self-esteem.

The two friends stare at the empty egg shells and discarded bones on the table. Every time this moment arrives, they realise they will both have to retreat to the corner of the room and take their places in the two old armchairs.

'Why do you insist on writing about a real-life woman?' the blood donor asks. 'It would be much easier to just make one up.' He rises to his feet, picks up the bottle of wine and takes it with him to one of the armchairs. There are still a few drops left in the bottle. The writer sinks into the other armchair, and they both lean their heads back against the wall. When two men are alone together, they often adopt this casual position to try to overcome their fear of intimacy. Without waiting for his friend to reply, the donor adds: 'I know you can't get her out of your mind. That slut. She deserved to die.'

'That's a terrible thing to say.' A look of rage flashes across the writer's swollen face.

'You two had broken up by the time I started going out with her. Or at least, you were having arguments all the time.'

'Is that what you call breaking up?' The writer remembers the day Su Yun told him she never wanted to see him again.

'Of course, I've always said it's best to break up with women gradually. After she dumped you, I advised you to stay away from her, but you continued to see her on the sly. That's how things were. We were all to blame.'

'So, what do you think is the best way to break up with a woman then?' the writer asks with a smirk. In his heart he knows that Su Yun's only motive for getting involved with them was to make the painter jealous.

'You should take her to a concert, or to the cinema.'

'Yes, but most of us can't manage that.' The writer looks away and thinks to himself: Su Yun and I were both following paths that were contrary to our nature, and in the end we had to return to the place we started from. Men keep their jealousy hidden, but women need to act it out. Was it us who destroyed her? Did she really exist? My memory of her is like a shard of broken glass that reflects back to me the occasional spark of love. 'Did you think she was pretty?' he asks after a long silence.

'No more pretty than any nice-looking woman you see walking down the street,' the blood donor says, lighting another cigarette. 'Women are very pragmatic. If you notice one standing before you with a cold, blank look on her face, you should leave her at once.'

'Her eyes never lied,' the writer says. 'Women's eyes only light up when they want you. Once they've got their hands on you, the light starts to fade.' The writer looks as though he has just emerged from a dark study. His eyes are glazed. The blood donor is used to this distracted manner of his. 'There's nothing so ridiculous as thinking love can be eternal,' the writer adds. 'Eternity is a bronze statue caked with green rust. Eternity is death.'

'We delude ourselves into thinking love will make us happy,' the blood donor replies. Suddenly the lights go out. In the dark, the men are like two smoking radio sets. The one on the left continues: 'We divide women up into the beautiful and the ugly. We only ever fall in love with a face.'

'So you really loved her then . . .' The man on the right sounds as dark and hollow as the wall behind him.

'I loved her in a different way from how you did. She said I was able to give her things you never could.'

'What things?'

'Do you have a motorbike? Do you have tickets for next week's concert? Do you have FECs? Can you take a woman into a hotel where foreigners stay? You have probably never even stepped inside the Friendship Store. Your year's salary isn't enough to buy one pair of Italian shoes. But look at me! Not only can I go into the Friendship Store and look at those Italian shoes, I can buy them with my own FECs. What do today's women want? The answer is everything that you don't have.' The voice on the left sounds as gravelly as a rusty bucket. 'Look, this cigarette lighter of mine is imported,' he adds, flicking it on with a *ttssaa.*

Four balls of light gaze at the foreign, blue flame. Then suddenly the flame goes out.

'How much did that cost you?' the voice on the right asks.

'It's filled with gas. If you meet a woman who smokes, just light her cigarette with it and she's yours.'

'We should think of women in the same way as we think of cigarette lighters,' says the voice on the right. This lighter of mine is too old, he thinks to himself. It's time I got myself a new one.

The two shadows fall silent in the black room. The darkness drags them back to their memories. A picture of the actress flashes before their eyes, or through their bodies.

The one on the left says: 'Sex is a good thing. It turns love into an action.'

'I don't think women attach more importance to sex than men. They are emotional creatures. If they feel no affection for you, their bodies become as hard as wood.'

'Not everyone can see things like you do. But if I could write, I'm sure I'd be a better writer than you. I know about the real world. You just write in order to fill your inner void, you have no experiences to draw from. You see life in terms of tragedy and myth. You are obsessed by your fear of death. But death is something everyone has to go through, there's nothing particularly interesting about it.'

'Corruption and secrecy have become the only laws in this country.'

'You could never keep to those laws,' the one on the left says. 'You just shut yourself up here, living in fear, blaming everyone else for your troubles. You would never dare jump into the thick of things and try to change your life, or to strive by any means possible to save yourself.'

'The law only protects those in power. The rest of us are doomed to play the victim.'

The Possessor *or* The Possessed

Every morning, he woke up beside his wife and counted the hours until his next adulterous tryst. The amorous longing seeped into his body like alcohol, allowing him to savour the numbness of his flesh and the trembling of various organs. He felt as though he were luxuriating in some magical Garden of Eden.

Had the textile worker not ruined everything, perhaps he could have gone on with his life – at least he would still be sitting behind that chief editor's desk of his, listening for the postman's footsteps that heralded the morning delivery of love letters that poured onto his desk like wine, ready for his slow delectation.

Ever since the editor of the town's bi-monthly literary magazine found this new way out in life, he would arrive at his office in the milky hours of morning, carefully make himself a cup of tea, pick up the hairs (mostly white and grey) that had fallen onto the desk, discreetly push the letters addressed to 'The Editor' to one side (note: there was no audience for these actions, he was performing them purely for himself), then through the corner of his eye he would scour the envelopes, searching for a handwriting he recognised or was waiting for. After rubbing a finger across the wrinkles at the corners of his eyes to remove the grains of dried mucus, his eyes and head would briefly dart in opposite directions, like a cat that deliberately looks away before it pounces on its prey. He would then remove his fashionable new leather shoes, pull open the lowest drawer of his desk to act as a footrest, and spread out a copy of the *People's Daily* to hide his bare feet from the view of anyone who happened to enter the room. Next, he would swing from side to side on his revolving chair, allowing his small body to create a satisfying level of noise, lean his head back on the chair's headrest and stare up at the ceiling. As his bony shoulders slowly relaxed, he would rub moisturising lotion into his hands, which were dry and wrinkled from years of cooking and washing-up, and only then would he finally begin to open the letters.

Sometimes, as the editor left the magical world of love letters and returned to real life, he would wink repeatedly and flutter his eyelashes. He had read that these exercises helped people regain their youthful demeanour, or at least gave their facial muscles an expressive tone. This was extremely important to a man over fifty who had only recently embarked on a secret love life. He often ground his teeth on his way to work, gnashing his jaws together in time with his steps. This exercise prevented him from falling into a daydream – and also improved his looks.

As soon as he opened the envelopes, he could tell from the handwriting whether it was a manuscript or a love letter. He had three drawers filled with love letters sent to him by young female writers. Some were from serious authors who simply wanted to be published; some from impressionable young girls hoping to fall in love; others were from young women whose respect for his literary talents had developed into an amorous infatuation. Over the previous two years, the editor had published in his magazine such poems as 'The Road in Life is Twisted', 'You Have Left Me, But I Cannot Leave You', 'Yet Another Sunset', 'An Autumn Leaf Blows Softly into the Window of My Heart', and had succeeded in having his way with each sentimental girl who had written them. He understood that to get young women to fall into his net, he only had to spout a few pompous statements on the meaning of life, and add a new column to his magazine entitled 'New People, New Poems'.

When selecting his prey, he always chose poetesses, and avoided female novelists like the plague. His life's experience had left him with a biological fear of female novelists. He made a point of insisting that everyone submitting a manuscript should enclose a photograph and curriculum vitae. Over the past two years, he had developed an expert ability to guess, just by looking at the handwriting and photograph, which woman would fall into his trap. Experience had taught him that plain women were usually the most talented, and that their gracefully written words often conveyed a sharp sense of observation. Women who wrote about blue skies, rosy clouds and fields of grass were the first to swallow his bait, but they usually had other men in the background and were fickle with their affections. He tended to focus his attention on the melancholy girls who liked to write about sunsets. Their poems invariably included references to wooden cottages in the snow, the last leaves of autumn, teardrops, 'that night he kissed me', and 'a cup of black coffee with no sugar'. Women of this category were average-looking, and since most of them came from troubled homes or had suffered heartbreak in the past, they harboured fantasies about a happy future. He knew how to exploit their weaknesses, and give them the kind of love they yearned for. They were used to being let down and deceived, so when the time came to cheat on them, they let go without a fuss. Apart from the young illustrator from the textile factory, who ended up clinging to him like a leech.

Mornings were an important time for him, and he devoted himself to his tasks with complete attention. By four in the afternoon though, his mind would drift into a series of fragmented and inconsequential dreams. (The professional writer considers that the editor's dreams were similar to the flights of fancy his own mind takes when the blood donor's conversation begins to tire him, or when his leader is chairing a meeting at the Writers' Association.) When he felt himself falling into a daydream, the editor would pretend to be reading the manuscript in his hand, his eyes skimming from one line to the next, or fixing on a particular sentence. His dreams were like a passer-by who just stays long enough to smoke a cigarette, then gets up and walks away.

One afternoon, he dreamed he was trudging through a river

of faeces. (The professional writer smiles to himself in his darkened room.) This image was no doubt a subconscious reaction to his excessive indulgence in romantic fantasies. He liked to weave into his dream a few flattering phrases from the love letters he received, bathing himself in a stream of compliments. 'You are the only man in the world,' he would hear the women whisper. 'A man of strength. The most important person in my life. I can't live without you.' 'You are a genius of unbridled talent, the great helmsman of the literary world.' He gained spiritual strength from these adulatory words, and for the first time in years, enjoyed a sense of self-respect.

He had once hoped to achieve this self-respect through his literary works. His wife, though, a professional novelist, succeeded in confining him to his role as husband, and he quietly entered his fortieth year at his post in the kitchen, surrounded by pots and pans. At first, this 'househusband', who was just 1.6 metres tall, tried to leave his daydreams during the brief intervals between washing the dishes and sweeping the floor, and conjure up an elegant phrase or two to jot down onto paper. But he soon gave up on that. Ten years later, he had to accept that all he was capable of was taking a few lines from one of his admirers' letters and sending them off to another. He knew he was merely the husband of the female novelist, and that any literary talent he'd had in the past was gone for ever.

He came from a family of intellectuals, his father was a doctor, his mother an actress in the local drama troupe. As a young man he had shown some talent. Three of his early poems were published in the *China Youth Daily*. He wrote an article about the achievements of Zhao Xianjin, a local hero who, like Lei Feng, gave money to the poor and helped old women across the road. It was published in the *Guangming Daily*, and made him as famous in this town as Zhao Xianjin himself. He was transferred from his menial job in a paper factory and placed in charge of propaganda at the People's Cultural Centre. His good fortune continued to grow. After seeing the Japanese film *Peach Blossom* about the reunion of a man and wife separated by war, he wrote a story called 'A Feeling for Home' about the reunion of a

Taiwanese man with his relations in China, and set it in this coastal town.

The story was immediately singled out for praise by the Central Committee's War Office, as it was very much in tune with their aspirations for national reunification. A film was commissioned, and the Central Committee sent to the town a team of production assistants and advisers, as well as ten actors, two of whom came from abroad. During the few days of filming, he became the most sought-after man in town, and when the municipal leaders bumped into him on the street, their speech took on a deferential tone. Everyone was talking about his script and the 'visitors from beyond the sky' that would soon flock to the town. When he walked through the streets, crowds would form behind him, strangers stopped him to say hello as though he were a visiting dignitary. In the evening, his home was surrounded by the same hordes of curious onlookers who loiter outside the big hotels where movie stars stay.

The proof of those glorious days was still in his home: a photograph of himself and the group of visiting actors that included the two foreigners. At the time, it was the only colour photograph in town. Unfortunately the photograph was taken in hospital – he had the misfortune to contract hepatitis just as the film was going into production. He was very flattered that the foreigners paid him a visit. After his meeting with them, he became the town's authority on all things foreign. When people who had only seen the foreigners from the front or behind, or who had only caught a glimpse of their hair or trousers, started arguing among themselves, someone would always end the dispute by saying, 'If you don't believe me, go and ask Old Hep.' (It was they who coined his nickname.) When the hospital's director was suspended for claiming that not all foreigners with black hair are mixed race, Old Hep's photograph saved him, because it clearly showed that one of the foreign actors had jet-black hair. Although the authorities demoted him to the less important position of chairman of the operating theatre, they at least allowed him to retain his Party membership.

In that golden year of his, the female novelist – his future wife

– sent a love letter to him in hospital. She called him 'China's Pavel', after Pavel Gorrchagin, the hero of a Soviet propaganda film. She said he was the sun around which she revolved, the shore on which she longed to moor her boat. It was the first time Old Hep had received a piece of paper inscribed with the petit-bourgeois phrase 'I love you'. He immediately passed the letter to the head of the Municipal Propaganda Department who had come to visit him in hospital. After a thorough investigation by the Party organs, he was informed that she was the daughter of the political commissar of the local army regiment. In under a week, the Party organs gave Old Hep their permission to embark on a relationship with her. They were also kind enough to return the letter to him, having made sure, of course, to draw a black line through every unhealthy, petit-bourgeois word it contained.

So she started to pay him visits. Had he not been suffering from a fever at the time, Old Hep might have noticed that the skirt she was wearing was identical to the one the actress Zhao Xiaohong had worn on her last visit to the town.

She sat down opposite him, her bare white legs dotted with goosebumps. 'All the nurses and female visitors seem to be wearing those skirts,' he remarked.

His future wife replied, 'These skirts have been around for ages. These days, everyone in the streets is wearing Zhao Dashan's jacket.'

'Who's Zhao Dashan?' he asked.

'An actor. You know, the big stocky one.'

'I can never remember their names,' Old Hep admitted guiltily.

'Even my little brother has heard of him!' She couldn't forgive Old Hep his ignorance.

Before she left his hospital room, she would always leave a few things behind to ensure that she remained in his thoughts. She left books inscribed with affectionate messages to him, discarded pear cores, the lingering fragrance of her talcum powder, a strand of her hair. He knew she was the daughter of a high-ranking Party cadre, and was overwhelmed by his unexpected stroke of good luck. The great disparity in their social standing inevitably caused him to review his own attributes: he was thirty-six years old, a Party member, earned a monthly salary of forty-seven and a half yuan, and had once been awarded the title of 'advanced worker' by his leaders at the paper factory. These details probably meant little to her. He knew that his professional success, however, would impress her more. He was the original screenwriter of the film *Feelings for Home*; he had managed to get nearly 200,000 words of material published by the *China Youth Daily* and *Guangming Daily*; on the strength of years of private study, he had been transferred from his menial job in the paper factory to a cadre's post in the People's Cultural Centre; he had driven in the municipal leader's red-flagged car, and had represented his paper factory on a visit to Beijing to meet the famous model worker, the 'Iron Man', Li Guocai. Everyone in town knew about these achievements. Although the female novelist had grown up in a home with five rooms and two toilets, her salary was no higher than his, and besides, she had only visited Beijing once, and that was as a child. Thinking this over in his mind, Old Hep felt a little more at ease. When he inhaled her fragrance in the air after her next visit, he felt a sudden surge of passion, and lying down on his hospital bed, he made up his mind to marry her.

A few months later, Old Hep took her as his wife, and soon after was appointed editor-in-chief of the Cultural Centre's new bi-monthly literary magazine. He had reached the peak of his career. But his luck was not to last, and in less than two years, his wife quickly caught up with him. Two of her novels were published by the most respected national journals, and she was suddenly proclaimed a 'regional and municipal talent'. She made visits to Beijing and Huangshan for two separate literary festivals. The month she and Old Hep were invited to join the newly established Literary Union, she alone was chosen by the authorities to be the town's first 'professional writer'. The government paid her a monthly salary so that she could stay at home all day writing novels. This turn of events didn't suit Old Hep at all. His wife stopped referring to him as 'China's Pavel', and started calling him Old Hep like everyone else. She made contact with other professional writers around the country, and became an authority on the latest cultural developments. She knew the name of the girlfriend of the Beijing writer Tan Fucheng, and was aware that the novelist Li Tiesheng had a paralysed leg. When the Open Door Policy was launched, she proved to be a fearless trailblazer of reform. She was the first woman in town to wear a padded bra, dye her hair and perm it like a foreigner. She read the daringly realist novel *Form Teacher* by Liu Xinwu, and the literary journal *Today* that was sent down to her from Beijing. She also took to composing romantic, melancholy verse. By the time Old Hep had finally managed to write the word 'love' down on a piece of paper, she was already using phrases like 'sexually aroused'. She corresponded with various young Beijing poets, sent them affectionate cards, and in return received letters in which they addressed her as 'my little lamb', 'my far-away treasure', and 'the angel wafting through my dreams'. She was completely in step with the fast pace of reform.

One night, Old Hep was leaning over his copy of *Selected Writings from Modern Western Literature* and about to doze off when his wife returned home from a party. He looked up and in the dim light saw, to his horror, a pair of hands with long red nails. He was terrified. At the time he felt the fear was more than his fragile body could stand. She looked down at him serenely, then glanced at her hands and said, 'It's nail varnish, you fool. Don't tell me you've never seen nail varnish before!'

'Blood-stained hands!' The hairs on the back of his neck were standing on end.

'Nail varnish!' she snapped angrily. 'All the foreign actresses in the glossy magazines have red nails. Haven't you seen?'

The image of blood-stained hands slowly retreated from his mind. It didn't worry him that he had never seen, or heard of, anyone painting their nails before. He knew he was incapable of keeping up with the pace of change. Trying to make up to her he asked: 'And why do they paint them red?' His voice sounded frail and sad.

'To make their hands look pretty, you idiot!' The novelist was angry. She could not tolerate this man who was frightened by her lipstick and nail varnish. She vowed never again to discuss modern cosmetic products with him.

Soon afterwards, she bought herself a pair of shoes with kitten heels, and started wearing her hair loose. Then she progressed to wearing stilettos, smoking foreign cigarettes, discussing Hemingway, drinking beer, spraying perfume on her neck, and celebrating her birthdays with a cake and candles. She boarded the Open Door Policy's express train, and soon she had read every translation of Milan Kundera's books, equipped her home with running hot water, a door bell, a telephone line, and arranged decorative ornaments and toys behind the glass front of her new bookcase. She was a fully-fledged modern woman. But it was a full decade later before Old Hep finally got round to reading *The Catcher in the Rye* and *One Hundred Years of Solitude*, watching a pornographic video, taking a mistress and buying a Western suit.

Since his wife was so much more at home with the climate of reform, he always ended up feeling excluded. The female novelist took him to parties, but Old Hep was conscious that he was short and unattractive and lacked any sense of rhythm. So when the disco music started, he would tremble with fear and retreat into the corner, staring miserably at the men and women cavorting before him. His wife even started meddling with his magazine. She turned up at his office to check manuscripts and commission pieces, and he would have to bow to her decisions. At home, she was the only one who received visitors. Her friends would drop in to engage her in literary discussions. As he listened in from the kitchen, Old Hep would hear them spout streams of unfamiliar terms such as 'linguistic weight', 'spherical structure', 'fragmentary style'.

On their third wedding anniversary, his wife's name entered *The Great Dictionary of Chinese Writers*, and he knew that from then on, he would have to assume the role of clown. That night, his wife invited a crowd of young admirers to the flat to celebrate her good fortune. A long-haired youth dragged Old

Hep out of the kitchen and demanded to hear his opinion on some issue or other. Old Hep stood in the centre of the room, lost for words. He looked up through the forest of guests, and saw his wife's face redden with rage. In a panic he said, 'Ask my wife. She's much more intelligent than me.' The guests laughed. He heard his wife whisper to him, 'What kind of man are you?' He had never heard her speak so softly to him before.

He shuffled back into the kitchen, humiliated and depressed. The guests roared with laughter. He hung his head low and arranged a few cabbage leaves around a plate of shredded tofu. He knew that if he had walked off towards the toilet instead of the kitchen, he would have made a more honourable exit, and exposed himself to less abuse from his wife once the guests had left.

He soon gave up all hope for a happy future and began to seek refuge in his daydreams. Whenever his wife rebuked him, he escaped into his fantasy world. After she entered the dictionary, it seemed to him that she had grown taller by half a head.

When she reached her forties, the female novelist's face, which had depended on youth for its appeal, suddenly took on the long gourd-like shape of her father's. Looking at it straight on, one could see through the make-up that the skin covering the more frequently-used facial muscles was now loose and wrinkled. But her body was still firm – a result of the confident posture she had adopted after being awarded Party membership at the age of eighteen. Her heavy bones and broad shoulders were clearly inherited from her military father.

Her temper grew worse with age. Whenever Old Hep did something to annoy her, she would twist his arm behind his back, flay her hand in the air like a kung-fu actress and kick him in the shins. His ignorance of cultural matters became the focus of her anger, and she was horrified when he finally admitted to being baffled by the new genre of 'Misty Poetry'. At the dinner table, he would hear his wife and her young guests discuss 'structuralism', 'low-flying aircraft narrative' and 'sickroom mentality', terms he couldn't find in the dictionary. Before he discovered that he was capable of taking mistresses, all he could do was listen respectfully and stare at his wife as she held forth.

When the beer and foreign nicotine reached her bloodstream, her speech and facial expressions became more animated. Feeling crushed by the vibrant tone of her voice, he would often seek comfort from a daydream. He could divide his dreams into separate parts like a string of sausages, cutting off in between one scene and the next to fetch a plate of radishes from the kitchen or to pour out more tea for the guests. As long as his wife didn't shout for his attention, his dream could continue episode after episode.

As his status in the home sank lower and lower, he realised that only in the kitchen could he feel free and act as he pleased. He could hurl bottles of rice vinegar on the floor without having to ask for their permission; he could slam his cleaver onto the chopping board whether there was meat lying on it or not. He could even kill things on this board. Transforming living creatures into dead creatures became his favourite pastime. When he gazed down at a chicken he had just beheaded struggling feebly in his hands, the troubles that plagued him in the outside world vanished from his mind. The instant the living animal became a dead corpse, he would scream a torrent of obscenities. One day, he pressed a live carp onto his board, thrashed his cleaver down and shouted 'Stinking hag!' as the head fell onto the cement floor.

Before he knew he was capable of taking mistresses, the only way he could escape his wife's control was to sink into a daydream. When he lay down in bed beside her, giving her one of the face massages outlined in her copy of *A Learner's Guide to Cosmetic Massage*, he would calm his mind with a dream about purple dustbins. It was a dream he indulged in quite regularly, and that seemed to alter slightly each time he had it. To find the dustbin, he had to travel a hundred metres in space-time, turn four corners, skirt a wall caked in flaking white ash, weave down an alley dotted with heaps of charcoal briquettes, pass a beer stall, a children's bookstore, two private restaurants, a shop selling burial clothes (a shiver always ran down his spine when he saw the mural showing dead corpses rising to heaven in a swoon), until he at last reached the purple dustbins at the back of the bicycle parking lot. Sometimes he would see his father pop out from one of the bins, remove his glasses, and peer at him with a sneaky look in his eyes. He knew that in thirty years' time, he would look identical to this man, only without the glasses.

When he had this dream several years later, the dustbin ended up boarding a plane. He was standing on a bus at the time, having spent an afternoon of passion with his young mistress in a ruined factory by the sea. The bus was jolting from side to side. While his body was still weak from the ejaculation and his heart still beating fast, he pulled the purple dustbin out of the plane and dragged it down into the ocean. The dustbin then became a mass of white manuscript paper drifting through his head. 'Like birds in flight,' he murmured as he returned to his senses.

('I like being around unhappy people,' the blood donor says.

The writer remembers that the man sitting beside him was once famed for his ability to pass wind. In the re-education camp, he once farted thirty-six times in one day. The writer also recalls how his friend bought a handful of lice off a villager for five yuan, then hid them under the quilt of Commander Li to punish him for snoring so loudly in his sleep.

He's capable of anything, the writer thinks to himself. But he's never had any success with women. He doesn't know how to treat them. All our old friends from the camp are married with children now, but he's still single. Surely he must get lonely! The writer's mind returns to the female novelist. During the Cultural Revolution, she was sent to a camp only eight kilometres away from theirs. She fell in love with Huang Gang there. He was a handsome young activist, the son of an ambassador, apparently. She and Huang Gang were the first couple in the area brave enough to live together without getting married. When they heard that the camp's leaders were about to send the militia to arrest them on charges of illegal cohabitation, she went directly to the headquarters and threatened to kill herself if any of them laid their hands on her. There was a Communist Party membership badge with a picture of

Chairman Mao pinned to her lapel at the time, so no one in the camp dared take the matter any further.

In her mind, Huang Gang was a modern-day Marx, and she was his Jenny, his political aid and lover. Had Huang Gang not been committed to a mental hospital a few years later, perhaps they would have married eventually, and she wouldn't have ended up with the wretched editor. The only purpose the editor served her now was to act as a contrast to her own success. What she longed for, though, was a man of steel, a hero or Jesus figure, so that she could take on the role of a protective tigress, or of a spoilt, attention-seeking child. When the Marx she was infatuated with was toppled from his position by a rival clique, she immediately fell from grace. With no man in her life to order her about, she became embittered and arrogant.

Then she met the editor and fell in love. But soon after she married him, she discovered, to her dismay, that he was a weak and feeble character, and she longed all the more for a man who could strike her with a whip, then gently wipe away her tears. Her drive to find a new man propelled her out of the flat and into the arms of her admirers. She looked for things in other men that the editor couldn't give her. One night, after one too many drinks, she visited the professional writer's flat with a look of despair in her eyes. The writer understood that, having been raised by a strict Communist cadre, she was ill equipped to deal with the torments of love. He knew that despite her flamboyant exterior, her heart was empty.

'We're beyond salvation. There's nothing any of us can do to help,' the writer mumbles to himself in the dark.

'I like to be with unhappy people,' the blood donor repeats.

'No one in this world is truly happy.' The writer is still thinking about the female novelist and the editor.)

When winter was setting in, Old Hep would start dreaming about apples. He would burrow through the sweet juicy fruit like a worm, gorging himself on the ripe flesh, carving out paths in all directions, then smearing his excreta onto the walls with the tip of his tail, leaving dark brown tunnels behind. All he wanted was to eat, then lie down quietly to digest. Nobody could interfere with him inside the fruit, and since apples are meant to be eaten, they raised no objections either. He moved in wide circles around the core, occasionally breaking through the peel. For some reason, he was convinced that the capital lay at the core, and he was afraid to approach it. He suspected that Chairman Mao and the senior cadres of the Central Committee lived there. As long as he kept clear of the core, he felt free to eat and wander at his will. In the world of the juicy apple, he at last found some peace and contentment.

'Is this not Communism?' he often chuckled to himself, as he lay in bed next to his wife who was unaware of the dream he was having. His dreams were not always so enjoyable, though. Every year on National Day, he would dream he was climbing a silk-cotton tree that was circled by loaves of golden bread. He knew that if he didn't control himself, he would end up scaling the trunk for ever. One night, as he reached for the highest branch, his wife shouted, 'Get off me, you bastard!' He woke to find himself clutching her hair. He quickly smoothed it back in place and fell asleep again, although he was too afraid to continue his dream.

It wasn't until he had served eleven years as editor that Old Hep discovered the true worth of his position. By the end of the summer, he was neglecting his professional duties and focusing all his attention on finding women. Before his visit to a Beijing literary conference held by the Ministry of Culture that spring, he could never have contemplated the possibility that he might one day take a mistress. But at the conference, he met a poetess from Shijiazhuang who, just like his wife, smoked cigarettes and painted her nails red, and was even a Party member too. She was shorter than his wife, however, and had finer bones. During the official speeches, he kept glancing in her direction to check the expression on her face. On the first night, when he was walking along the hotel corridor on his way to the men's bathroom, the poetess stuck her head around her door and called out to him. Her lights were on, but when he stepped inside her room, she switched them off and wrapped her arms around him. Her tender kisses soothed his nerves, and in less than a minute, his legs stopped shaking.

Two years later, he realised that ever since that night, he had tried to find in other women the sour, sooty smell that infused her hair and the inside of her cotton knickers. That night in Beijing, he learned that he too was capable of committing sinful acts. He said to himself, If a woman is willing to give her body to me, who am I to turn her down?

The following morning, the delegates convened in the conference room and continued their analysis of articles on the political rectification of cultural and artistic troupes. As Old Hep sat in his seat, he felt himself grow bigger and taller. He was wallowing in the joy of entering the sweet apple of Communism. His voice became fluid and natural. As he rose to deliver his speech, the poetess's naked bottom flashed through his mind. He slowly removed the flowery knickers. Two plump, white buttocks . . .

'There are no words to express the greatness of Chairman Mao's thoughts on literature and art,' he summed up at the end of his speech. 'They are simply amazing!'

He returned home a different person. He was now a man of courage, a man who could possess other women.

Before the summer was over, he asked a girl from the local textile factory who was drawing some illustrations for his magazine whether she would like to go out on a date with him, and she accepted. So he took her to the woods behind Red Scarf Park. They sat on a bench and she sketched the golden sunset reflected on the surface of the lake. The water was calm and the air was filled with buzzing insects. The editor, who was now in his late forties, stood behind the girl and breathlessly stared at her delicate ear, and the small hand that was continually hooking a lock of hair behind it. He knew that every young woman in town dreamed of finding a permanent job in his editorial department, and that they regarded him as a successful and influential man. The textile worker had looked deeply flattered when he asked her out on this date. Indeed, he was everything she was looking for in a man. Fired with confidence, he rested his hand on the girl's shoulder and commented on the branches she was drawing. A blush rose to the girl's cheeks. Noticing the pencil start to shake in her hand, he moved in closer and wrapped his other arm around her. His balance was not good though, and as he leaned forward, his foot slipped, and he toppled awkwardly to the ground, bringing the girl down with him. He edged over, and without a word, climbed on top of her. She kept her eyes closed throughout, except at the moment of deepest pain, when she opened them briefly and looked into the sky, and saw the clouds turn from red to purple.

Following that successful tryst, he invited her to his office after work on several occasions, hoping to have his way with her again. She accepted every time, and before long became his first official mistress. The joy of possessing a woman, of possessing a virgin, gave him a new lease of life.

'Before you, I had only ever made love to my wife,' he told her, as he lay flat across her body.

'And before I met you, I was a virgin,' she replied, looking up with a smile.

'You have turned my life around,' the editor said, stroking her smooth forehead. 'I don't think of myself as middle-aged in the least. I'm only thirty-one years older than you, after all.'

The textile worker boosted the editor's confidence, and when this confidence spread to his professional life, women began to land on his desk like the manuscripts he received every day. As long as he agreed to publish their works, these women were ready to lay themselves down below his wrinkled body. All he had to do was choose his prey and drop a few subtle hints. He seldom had time to daydream, he was too busy dealing with the growing list of women with whom he was conducting illicit affairs. His secret happiness lent his expression an air of maturity. Nobody knew that when he was chairing the political education meetings at work, or doing the washing-up at home, he was, in his mind, climbing onto a woman, thrusting her legs in the air and subjugating her to his will.

He began to notice the differing ways women behaved during their moments of greatest pleasure. The textile worker paled in comparison with the women who succeeded her. At the peak of her excitement, all she did was let out a soft croak. She never groaned or moaned, or moved her legs about like the more mature women. One woman who stuck most in his mind was a short-story writer from Sichuan. He could never forget the sight of her long dancer's legs coiled around his elderly body. Unfortunately, once he had published her work, she dropped him like a brick. She proved to be, however, the most memorable woman of all the twenty-one he slept with. In his treasured pink notebook he labelled 'Compendium of Beauties', he made a careful record of her birthday, her shoe size and address.

At home, Old Hep became more relaxed, and started to pay more attention to his wife, who had recently brought out her sixth book. (When the professional writer remembers the story of 'Marx' and 'Jenny' in the novel that made her famous, he is overcome with nausea. Her thinly-veiled autobiographies reek of the fetid regurgitations of her past.) The pockets of Old Hep's suit were filled with name cards emblazoned with his professional titles of 'editor-in-chief' and 'Director of the Writers' Association'. Whenever he met someone for the first time, he would ceremoniously present a card to them with a serious, yet approachable, look on his face. His small stocky build gave people the impression that he was a reliable, hardworking man. After all these years of waiting, he had at last boarded the express train of the Open Door Policy.

After he published the first novel of a local young writer he had discovered (a book the critics later declared to be China's most avant-garde work of fiction), he gained the respect and admiration of the town's young literati. They praised his astute eye for talent, and delivered urgent requests to make his acquaintance. To prepare himself for his meetings with them, Old Hep spent many hours trying to learn the phraseology and tone of voice that his wife employed during her literary discussions. Soon he too was able to pepper his speech with terms like 'the collective subconscious', 'twilight mentality', 'the absurd' and 'pseudo-realism'.

For a while, the female novelist felt left out, and sank into a mild depression. She seemed to have lost the upper hand. When they received visits from women writers who were just like she was twenty years before, she appeared sallow and lacklustre in comparison. Although the new generation of women painted their nails the same shade as hers, they chose to wear not red, but mauve or fluorescent pink lipstick. The fact that she had dared to wear tight jeans a decade before, and had even been prepared to write a self-criticism about it, meant very little to these young women who now preferred to dress in baggy jeans and imported trainers. The most forward-thinking women had already visited Shenzhen and returned with tight, wiry perms. When Old Hep's wife started sounding off about Hemingway's *The Old Man and the Sea*, the young women drifted to the corner of the room to discuss Heidegger and Robbe-Grillet. Her favourite topic of conversation – her memories of the Cultural Revolution and life in the re-education camp – meant nothing to them. They treated her with the detached indifference with which they would treat anyone else from their parents' generation.

('We're finished,' she told the professional writer when she visited his room one night, half drunk. 'This generation knows nothing about suffering, or isolation. Their hearts are numb.'

'And what good does isolation bring?' the writer asked.

'They just don't take life seriously.'

'Neither did you, at their age.'

'Writing demands complete sacrifice. You must pour your soul into the work. Every word has to be paid for in sweat and blood.'

'But if you cut yourself off from today's world, how can you hope to write about it?' the writer said.

'Writers are the products of their times. A shallow world produces shallow writers. I can't help missing those years we spent in the re-education camps.'

'The world has moved on,' the writer said. 'You've been left behind. Those young women understand today's society better than you. Perhaps a purer form of literature will emerge from their numb minds. They have no prejudices, no interest in politics. Their problems are purely personal. But you . . . your time is already over.')

Old Hep's passion for the textile worker gradually waned like a poplar tree in autumn, losing more and more leaves with each gust of wind. These winds were caused, of course, by the editor's increasing number of lovers. The textile worker put up with his neglect, and didn't lose hope. She believed that her love would finally conquer him, so she stuck to his side and refused to let go. But he only ever agreed to meet her when there was no other prey available. He was determined to live life to the full and make use of all the opportunities his job gave him. He had gained confidence from the textile worker's adoration, and courage from the advances of the Sichuanese short-story writer. (Although, when the Sichuanese woman had said things like 'Unhook my bra' or 'I love your little bald patch', he had trembled with fear.) He knew that in order to progress, he needed to continue having these amorous experiences.

The textile worker had been raised in a strict household. Her mother was a government functionary who stuck religiously to the Party rules, her father had died in hospital during the Cultural Revolution. She was an only child, and to support her mother, she had started work as soon as she graduated from high school. If she had gone to university, she would have had to leave town, and her mother would never have agreed to that. So she learned to content herself with what this town could offer her. She knew that if she behaved well in the textile factory, she might be promoted to an office job, and from there perhaps be transferred to a job in the People's Cultural Centre. She longed to leave the clanking looms behind and find herself a quiet desk job. The editor became her role model. He had told her that as a factory worker he had studied creative writing in his spare time, and on the back of his first film script was promoted to his job as editor-in-chief. When she gazed at him, his short little body seemed Napoleonic, his bloated and lined face reminded her of Beethoven. Having grown up with no paternal love, she looked upon him as a father figure. She only had one aim in life, and that was to remain by his side for ever.

Unfortunately, as soon as she gained possession of him, her joyous mood caused a dramatic improvement in her appetite. The fat she acquired attached itself first to her waist and calves, then spread to her face, puffing her upper eyelids and inflating her cheeks. After two years together, the editor could no longer bring himself to look at her. She had lost all her girlish charm, and now had the body of a middle-aged woman. The other mistresses he had taken subsequently put her in the shade. He was ashamed of her, and longed to free himself from her ties. One Wednesday afternoon, he agreed to meet her behind Red Scarf Park, hoping to use this opportunity to break up with her once and for all.

(Relations between people are very curious, the writer reflects. We behave kindly, even sycophantically towards people we are afraid of, but trample like tyrants over the shy and retiring. Our roles are determined by our opponents. We all possess a dual nature. The editor was a servant to his wife, a master to the textile worker – roles he couldn't play with any of his other women. We all jump from one role to the next. If I continue to write this story, who knows, the textile worker might become more savage even than the female novelist.)

By the time she finally turned up in the woods behind Red Scarf Park, Old Hep was seething with rage. He had never felt like this before. On the way to this rendezvous he sensed that a physical change was about to take place in him. She ran towards him, her plump body wobbling about as though she were being tossed up and down inside a rattling old car. She apologised for being late, but he continued to glare at her. Her cheeks turned red with remorse. In fact, at this point, she should have thrown herself onto his chest, as she used to in the past, and quashed the fire in his body with the weight of her womanly flesh. But the cold, heartless expression on his face sapped her confidence, and she dared not reach out to him.

Old Hep was pleased by the turn of events, however. Her lateness allowed him to keep his anger on the boil, and when he saw her cowering below him with a pathetic look on her face, he knew he was ready to explode. (Unattractive women should never stand still in front of a man if they want to win him over. They should first arch their eyebrows gracefully, amuse him with a funny anecdote, or smother him with kisses – anything to divert his attention away from their piggy eyes or pointed chin. This is admittedly very tiring, but it must be done. Everybody must learn to do the best with what they've got.) The rage must have been simmering inside him for years, because without a second's hesitation, he was able to lift his hand in the air and bring it down hard on her face.

'Stupid bitch!' he shouted after the first blow. 'Why are you late?'

He had learned these gestures and tone of voice from his wife. During their childless married life, she had shouted at him once in this way, when the jumper he had washed for her and hung out to dry on the balcony was blown away by the wind. She accused him of having done it on purpose, and when he replied that the jumper was so wet that he'd had no choice but to hang it up outside, she slapped him on the face. At the time, he sensed some organ in his body shift place a little. He ran into the kitchen, grabbed a ladle of cold water and emptied it into his mouth. He drank until he was dizzy. Today he returned that slap. Although he had trouble speaking at first, and his voice sounded like a shovel grating against an iron bucket, he soon loosened up. His hand had struck her right on the face. He had succeeded. His confidence rising, he punched her in the chest, and she fell to the ground at the very spot on which she had lost her virginity. The actions she took next decided her fate. Instead of hitting back, she struggled to her knees and pleaded for forgiveness.

In Old Hep's mind, her supplicant pose affirmed the correctness of his behaviour. He abandoned all sense of restraint. At last he was making up for all those lost years.

As dusk gave way to night, Old Hep felt an uncontrollable

urge to possess her. He climbed on top of her and took command of her weak and feeble body. She clenched her teeth and croaked as he bit her nipples and tugged her hair. Although she was taller than him, each time she struggled to her feet he managed to kick her down again.

'Will you leave me alone now?' he shouted.

'I'll do anything to make you happy,' she answered, gazing up at him adoringly before collapsing again onto the grass.

'Haven't I made myself clear?' he said, pulling up his trousers. 'I never want to see you again!' Then he spat on the ground and walked away.

(Suddenly the lights come back on in the eighth-floor flat. What is love exactly? the writer asks himself. He glimpses a cloth doll slumped in the corner of his room, and wonders what it's doing there. He often catches sight of it, although he usually suspects his eyes are playing tricks on him, because he only ever sees it at night, or when he's drunk or lost in thought. Perhaps there really is a cloth doll under the chair. Maybe it was given to him by some woman, or left behind by a friend. Or perhaps the previous occupant of the flat flung it in the corner in a fit of anger. No one has ever bothered to lean down and pick it up. The dirtier the doll gets, the less willing he is to touch it.)

The editor's drawers were filled with love letters. Because this town is built beside a deep-water port, it was one of the first places to benefit from the relaxed trade regulations of the Open Door Policy. As its economy flourished, the town grew and a new urban district was constructed on the farmland that lined the coast. Hordes of peasants from inland villages poured into this district to sell their produce and search for new jobs. Soon everyone in China had heard of this town, and the name of Old Hep's literary magazine grew in prestige. He was happy with his job. His colleagues in the editorial department regarded him affectionately. In the political study sessions, his fellow Party members admired his open-minded opinions and his courage in giving voice to minor grievances. The new recruits looked up to him; when chatting with them, he would always drop words like 'sexy', 'contemporary' and 'tasteful' into his conversation to make them feel at ease. He knew that as long as the textile worker didn't decide to cause any more trouble, he could remain safely in his post until retirement. He racked his brains, thinking of ways to get rid of her. Since she had lost all her self-respect, he knew he could torture her as he wished. As the weeks passed, he discovered that he enjoyed tormenting her, and since she was a willing victim, they ended up seeing more of each other than ever.

He was aware that it was he who had fallen for her first. On her first day in his office, he told her about how hard he was working on his novel, and about the chess competitions he'd won at school. He presented himself as a man who had suffered much in life, and who was in desperate need of consolation. When the textile worker glanced up at him, there was no love in her eyes. But she needed a father figure, and was flattered that the editor was paying her so much attention – no man had shared such intimate thoughts with her before. So when he wrapped his arms around her in the woods behind the park, she didn't push him away. For a while everything was fine, they satisfied one another's needs. The textile worker wasn't wrong to fall in love with Old Hep, her mistake was to cling to him after he had moved on to his next prey. Her love for him destroyed her.

Each time Old Hep tried to break up with her, she said she would only agree on condition he gave her a baby before they separated. This demand crushed his spirit, and he soon resumed his habit of escaping into daydreams.

Although the editor still walked to work each morning with rosy cheeks and an eager smile, he would now return home with an ashen face. After he entered his flat, he would remove his shoes, sink into his sofa and start dreaming he was hauling furniture around the room. Sometimes a heavy jujube chair weighed down on him so heavily that his head dripped with sweat. One day, as smells of boiled chicken bones wafted from the kitchen, he dreamed he was dislodging a huge fitted unit from the wall. When he woke up a few minutes later, stirring the chicken soup, he felt a sudden urge to smash the unit on the head of the boorish two-bit writer from the provinces who was showing off to his wife in the living room, then grab his lousy novel and tear it to shreds. Instead, he diluted the beer with water and sprinkled sand over the rice before he carried the meal next door. Then he watched his wife and the guest wince as their teeth grated against the sand. His legs trembled with excitement. He swore that if that wretched writer stayed one more day in their flat, he would dilute the beer with piss.

But at home, he was still a servant, always having to check the expression on his wife's face before making a move. She ordered him about with the ferocity of a tigress, and he did as he was told. After completing his marital duties, he would squeeze the sperm from his condom, as she requested, and smear it over her face and thighs. (She'd read in a magazine that the most expensive French face cream was manufactured from sperm, and always insisted that Old Hep rub the entire contents of his condoms into her skin.) When he was with the textile worker, he was able to ejaculate into her mouth then demand she swallow every drop.

'On my face!' the tigress growled, as the editor climbed back onto the bed and leaned over her. Old Hep noticed that there was very little sperm in his condom, and put it down to the secret tryst he'd enjoyed the day before. As he carefully rubbed the remaining drops onto his wife's face, he cursed inwardly: 'You ugly old bat. Your face is as furrowed as the fields of Dazhai.'

He kept rubbing until the sperm had dried onto her skin like white face powder. 'I could do what I liked with her,' he said to himself. 'She let me grab her tits and suck them dry. Hers were much whiter and softer than yours.' When he got out of bed to wash his hands, he felt his empty testicles begin to warm again.

Once he started taking mistresses, he was no longer plagued by his recurring dream about tipping truckloads of earth into the sea. But when the textile worker said she would only break up with him on condition he gave her a child, he once again stepped into the cabin of the huge truck, and looked through his rear mirror at the mounds of earth dropping into the waves of the ocean. During his afternoon break in the editorial office, he would drive the truck back and forth in a daze. His colleagues would notice him staring at the wall, smiling, then frowning at the calendar that was already two years out of date. They knew that he was sinking into a daydream, and they would take advantage of this time to slip off to buy a snack or make a telephone call.

When he was in this dream state, his colleagues could tell what he would be capable of doing from the different expressions on his face. If he was frowning, he would still be able to hear the telephone and look at his manuscripts; he could even stand up, shake hands with a visitor and pace about the room. But when he woke up, he would forget everything that had happened. When his lips curled into a faint smile, the most he could do was rise from his seat, walk to the thermos flask and empty some hot water into his cup. He alone knew that at this point the truck he was driving was moving with particular speed and agility. However, when the truck started racing across the surface of the sea and was about to carry him into the blue sky, his expression became deadly earnest, and his eyes would fix on some distant point. Sub-editor Chen, who knew a few things about the art of Qigong, claimed that this was the look of a man gazing into eternity after emerging from a deep meditation.

'He's entered the realm of emptiness,' 'Old Qigong' explained to the art director who was attempting to grow a goatee. 'His soul has left his body. He's as dazed as you were that night you got drunk and pulled your trousers down.'

Although the editor's daydreams were very intense, they seldom lasted more than twenty minutes.

When it first became obvious that he was daydreaming at home, the female novelist made fun of him. 'Have you lost your ears, you moron?' she laughed when he failed to respond to her question. At that moment, he was staring at the crockery in the sink and the water gushing from the tap, while in his mind he was climbing a tree to pick from its branches the candyfloss he loved to eat as a child. When he failed to answer her a second time, his wife stormed into the kitchen, grabbed a carrot, and with the might of an army general, stabbed it into his back. Immediately, he leapt from the branches, crashed into the trunk, then landed in a confused heap on the kitchen floor. He woke up to find himself sprawled on a pile of potatoes, looking up at his wife with a ladle in his hands.

From then on, he was careful to dream with just one side of his brain, and use the other side to carry out his duties in the real world. Although he couldn't always avoid some overlap between one world and the other, he usually managed to keep things under control.

Then one day, the textile worker finally found her way to his flat. She had tried to follow him home for days, but since he always took a different route, she often lost track of him. Old Hep was not in when she knocked. She considered leaving straight away, but the female novelist could sense that something was up, and that the young woman was embroiled in some way with Old Hep. When she asked her how they knew each other, the textile worker burst into tears and refused to say a word. The novelist promptly shooed her away, and decided to wait until Old Hep's return before commencing her investigation.

'Did you sleep with that girl or not?' she asked her husband as he walked through the door.

He looked up at her with terror. He knew how fierce she could be, and knew that what stood behind her was even more ferocious. Her commissar father could beat the life out of him. He saw her standing before him, legs apart, as steady as a suspension bridge, and he confessed everything.

The textile worker was immediately interrogated by her leaders. They criticised her 'petit-bourgeois liberalism' and told her that she would be denied promotion for two years. Her supervisor took advantage of the situation and ordered her to straighten her perm and stop wearing flared trousers. The next day she turned up at the factory in plaits and baggy slacks. But her spirit was still strong, and as soon as she clocked off after lunch, she let her hair down again, put on some lipstick, and made her way to Old Hep's office.

'I don't care about anything any more,' she whined, as she chased him around his desk.

'If my wife catches sight of you again, my life will be over.' His leaders had passed by that morning to warn him to pay attention to his lifestyle. 'You must leave now. I have a meeting to go to,' he lied.

'But there's something I must tell you.'

She followed him out of the building. They walked through the crowd, one in front of the other, as though they were strangers.

'What did you tell your factory leaders?' he asked.

'I admitted that we've been sleeping together for years,' she said to the nape of his neck, desperately trying to keep up with him.

Old Hep felt as though his head were about to explode. His steps became heavy.

She followed him closely, refusing to fall behind. 'I'm not afraid of them.'

'Go away, will you, just go away!' he hissed through his teeth. She stood still for a moment, but he kept walking.

When he heard her catching up with him, he said: 'If I see you again, I'll kill you!' As he was about to run away, he heard something that made him stop dead in his tracks. He had clearly heard her utter the words: 'I'm pregnant!'

These words filled him with a mixture of grief and anger. 'Walk in front of me,' he said, without looking back. 'I'll meet you in our place behind the chemical plant.' Then he slowed down and watched her lumpish body overtake him then waddle away through the crowd towards the sea. His heart jumped. In the editorial department today, he had sensed that something was not right. He had recently taken a shine to a young student from a provincial university who attended his literary study classes at the Municipal Cultural Department. She had a large bottom, and a big round face that smiled all the time like a clay doll. When he'd telephoned the Cultural Department that

97

morning to ask her out for a date, the official who picked up the phone said she wasn't there. When he asked him to tell her to bring him the manuscript of her novel, the officer slammed the phone down. At the time, he just swore at the officer for being so rude, but now he realised that someone had been spreading rumours.

When his wife had informed the textile worker's leaders of the situation, they had promised to treat the case in confidence, but news had obviously leaked out. The bastards. Now everyone knew. As he trailed at a distance behind the textile worker's motherly frame, his legs seemed to grow weaker and weaker.

'So you want a baby now do you? Bitch!' he cursed under his breath, watching the textile worker advance through the crowd. His stomach felt heavy and swollen. He followed her down an alley and saw her disappear through a hole in the wall. He continued a few paces, deliberately passing the cavity, then turned back again and jumped in.

Standing inside the crumbling carcass of the abandoned factory, he could hear the waves of the sea bash against the cement embankment below. Sometimes when he came here, he could smell the rancid effluent that poured from the chemical plant behind, especially at dusk when the stench evaporated from the damp earth or was carried over in the evening breeze. In the sweltering heat of summer, the textile worker always brought a tin of tiger balm and gently rubbed the ointment onto Old Hep's wizened legs to keep the insects away. He could now hear her walking towards him, treading over the loose tiles that lay scattered on the ground. He liked this secret spot. Although it was infested with mosquitoes, the place was usually empty. Trucks from the suburbs would drive past on the road outside from time to time, and people occasionally jumped through the hole in the wall to have a piss in the yard, but no one ventured inside the ruined building. He and the textile worker always met in a room in the middle that had probably served as the factory's control centre. The three walls that were still standing reached slightly above their heads, and the floor was covered with a smooth layer of cement. When the diesel engine in the chemical plant next door shut down for the day, they would sit back and breathe the salty breeze, and imagine themselves in some beautiful seaside villa. He saw that the textile worker had pulled out the plastic sheet they kept in the corner under a brick, and was now sitting on it. On the crumbling wall behind her, a faded Maoist slogan read: WE MARCH FORWARD, FIRED BY OUR COMMON REVOLUTIONARY GOAL.

'Come and sit down,' she said to him softly.

'Sit down, you say!' Old Hep knew that the chemical plant hadn't yet closed for the day, so he was careful to keep his voice down. 'How did you manage to get pregnant? I haven't touched you for three months.'

'Well I am,' she said defiantly. 'It happened ages ago.'

They both set out their demands. Old Hep promised to find her a backstreet clinic that provided quick abortions for unmarried women. The textile worker said she would only agree to an abortion on condition that he continue to see her afterwards.

By the time dusk fell, they were still locked in argument. Old Hep's eyes glowered with rage. He leaned over and snarled, 'If you don't stop clinging to me, I can't be held responsible for my actions.'

The textile worker looked up at him calmly from the plastic sheet. Her body was scarred with the wounds he'd inflicted on her in the past. A few months before, he had kicked her abdomen so hard she lost control of her bowels. She was still having to take medicine for it. Her stomach was also affected, and whenever she ate anything cold she suffered terrible cramps.

'Please sit down,' she said. 'I want to talk to you.' Her eyes looked sore. Today was her nineteenth birthday. She calculated that she had been with him for two years and seven months. Their love story had reached its 940th day. 'I wanted you to take me out to a restaurant tonight.' She stroked Old Hep's shoe and, sensing no resistance, proceeded to move her hands up his calf. She knew how to win him over. When he was in a bad mood, she only had to touch his flies and he would calm down and apologise to her. Because she was taller than him, she always made sure she was sitting down before she touched him, to give him a sense of superiority. Today, she crouched at his feet, then slowly climbed onto her knees. She looked up at him, offering her lips to his, but he pushed her head down to his opened flies, then grabbed her hair and thrust her head back and forth over his groin. Her stomach clenched, her throat was so filled with his engorged flesh she could barely breathe. At last his hands loosened their grip. She slumped to the ground, curled herself up on the plastic sheet and choked on the fluid in her mouth.

'Don't cough so loudly!' the editor yelled, pulling his trousers up.

Night had fallen by now. The white plastic sheet reflected the pale moonlight and scattered it softly over the girl's body. She tried hard not to vomit. Her puffed eyelids became even more swollen.

'You bitch!' the editor swore from the back of his throat. He seemed as though he were about to collapse. 'Are you satisfied now?' Ever since he had first slapped her on the face, he'd stopped whispering sweet words in her ear, or buying her collections of poetry. Instead, he'd taken to biting and pinching her, and when he saw her mouth contort with pain, he felt pleased and light-headed. She put up with his tortures, as though she were enduring some trial of love. Sometimes, if she was lucky, Old Hep would give her a quick cuddle afterwards to cheer her up. Tonight she was still waiting for this longed-for embrace.

The editor crouched down beside her and said: 'So you're getting an abortion. Is that settled then?'

'No,' she said, wiping the sperm from her face. 'I want you to take me out to a restaurant. It's my birthday today.'

'To hell with your birthday! Are you having that abortion?' He leaped to his feet and kicked her shins. 'Tell me – are you getting that abortion, or not?'

The textile worker remained silent and refused to surrender.

'Open your legs!' he shouted. The textile worker turned round and looked up at him. Her face was even paler than the moonlight. The editor kicked her in the stomach. She shuddered with pain, and pressed her hands over her abdomen. A howl roared from the pit of her stomach, but emerged from her throat as a timid hiss. Gasping for air, she retreated to the wall that bore Chairman Mao's slogan. The editor walked over to her and pinched her tear-drenched face.

'I'll stay with you until the day I die,' she moaned from somewhere deep inside her.

'Get an abortion first, then I'll listen to your crap.' The editor tried to adopt the authoritative tone he used when answering his subordinates' questions in the office. This tone of voice commanded obedience. It was used by his leader, his leader's leader, and every leader above him. Unfortunately, his throat was too narrow to replicate the husky and mellifluous tones produced by the secretary of the municipal Party committee.

'I'll give you a hundred yuan,' he promised, hoping that this would persuade her.

The textile worker was still trembling, her head bowed low. But when she heard those words, she broke into tears again and sobbed, 'Now that I've slept with you, I must stay with you for ever.'

'That's just what your mother's taught you,' he sneered.

'You said yourself that you didn't want me to go with any other man.'

'That was two years ago! I've been telling you for months that it's time you found another man and got married.'

'I can't! You're the only intellectual I know.'

'Some workers have a bit of culture too, if you look hard.'

'I only want a writer. If I'm not with a writer, my life will be over. I could never fall in love with an ordinary man. And as for your troubled past and unfortunate family background – they make me love you all the more.'

'I made all that up,' the editor confessed, kicking his skinny legs about nervously.

'I don't believe you. Why would anyone make up a story about being sent to prison?'

'I didn't really go to prison. I was arrested once by the Young

Pioneers during the Cultural Revolution, but nothing serious happened. They just locked me up in an office for a couple of hours.'

'Does that mean that your promotion to editor on the back of private study was invented as well?'

'All of it,' the editor laughed, gloating over her misfortune. 'I'm a nobody. A talentless fool!' he chirped, his legs now perfectly still. 'Just hurry up and tell me,' he added in a harsher tone, 'are you having that abortion or not?'

She paused for a moment, and said: 'I'm not really pregnant – I just wanted to see you, I wanted you to spend some time with me. Nobody pays me any attention at work, they all swear at me behind my back. Besides, it's my birthday today.' She lifted her face towards the moonlight. As the tears sparkled down her cheeks you could see hidden, behind her tangled fringe, two dark eyes filled with terror and love.

'You lied to me!' he spluttered. He imagined pounding her to death. The ground was littered with loose bricks and tiles. He considered drowning her – the sea was just a few minutes' walk away. He stared at her face. This steadfast, stubborn girl had drained him of all his energy. Nothing could shake her resolve. He grabbed a bunch of her hair and shouted, 'Open your mouth! Open it!'

As he unzipped his flies again, the textile worker opened her mouth, and staring blankly into the sky, she said, 'When you've had your piss, take me to a restaurant and buy me some birthday noodles. I beg you, just this once . . .'

At night, after he had massaged his wife to sleep, he would stare at the traces of lipstick around her gaping mouth, and think things through in his mind. It was a precious moment for him. Of course, it was impossible to write novels or poetry during this time, but at least he could relax and enjoy the rare minutes of freedom afforded by his wife's sleep. She was more talented than him, and came from a better family. The day he first met her his pulse had quickened a beat, and had only slowed down since then when he was asleep.

There was a reason for his fear. He had once witnessed his father-in-law, the political commissar, slap the female novelist on her face. The noise of this slap had reverberated through his head, almost causing him to lose his mind. After that, he was always petrified that his wife might decide to slap him in the same way. Before he first hit the textile worker, violence had terrified him. He had grown up in a quiet household that smelled of soap and Chinese medicine. His father was about the same size as him, maybe a little shorter, and had white, delicate hands which, when he moved them, looked as elegant as a lady's. He would never have dreamed of using them to hurt anyone. When his father was targeted during the Cultural Revolution, his family cut themselves off from others. Only his mother dared raise her voice at home. When she was happy, she would sing her favourite song – 'The Tibetan Serfs Sing with Joy at their Peaceful Liberation'. When his father returned from work, he would play cards and Chinese chess with him. Had it not been for the Cultural Revolution, Old Hep would have finished his university course, and would probably have been a university professor by now.

Usually, when he lay in bed beside his wife, he would try to disturb her sleep by pulling over the lamp and shining it on her wrinkled skin. He alone knew the reason why she always insisted on sitting in one particular armchair: it was because the light at that spot was the most flattering. One day she had sat in every seat in the room and asked Old Hep to tell her where the light was kindest to her complexion. When she sat in the armchair he'd chosen, she checked her face in her hand mirror and discovered that the light from the orange lamp beside her did indeed give her skin a serene and youthful glow.

Sometimes he would clench his fists and hiss as he looked down at the sleeping tigress. When she started to snore, he would run over in his mind the details of his secret flings. He was proud of having deceived his wife. He would smirk at the breasts that drooped to either side of her ribcage, and cup his hands over them to show how large his latest girlfriend's breasts were. 'They're *this* big,' he would whisper, the corners of his eyes wrinkling with glee. 'She's got tits this big, and you've just got two little ping-pong balls.'

But tonight Old Hep had lost his courage. All he could do was curl up into a ball, and in the dim light stare at the heap of flesh sprawled beside him. Before she fell asleep, the female novelist had warned him she would visit his work unit again the next day. She had already dropped by his department that afternoon, planning to tell Old Hep's leader about the affair and plead with him not to take the matter any further. She knew that if her father ever got wind of the situation, she and Old Hep would both be finished. But when she walked into Old Hep's empty office and discovered the huge stack of love letters hidden in his desk (she was able to prise the drawers open quite easily with the aid of an ordinary penknife), she immediately changed her mind. As the scale of his infidelities became clear, her first instinct was to kill him; her second was to spare his life, but ensure it was a miserable one; her third was to kick him out of the house and wipe him from her mind. After she had rejected the first and the third options, she set to work on the second.

She selected twenty or so love letters that displayed some literary skill, and put them aside to use later as material for her novels. She chose another twenty of the more intimate letters hidden in a notebook labelled 'Compendium of Beauties' – a pink exercise book with a picture of a house and a mushroom on the cover – swapped the letters around, scrawled 'return to sender' on every envelope and posted them back, so that a few days later each woman would receive a letter that another admirer had written to him. She collected all the sentimental letters from love-struck girls who hoped to conquer the editor with their youthful charms, and posted them to the Party committees of their respective work units. She summoned the leader of the People's Cultural Centre and made him dispatch official letters to the work units of over seventy other women who'd written to her husband, demanding they conduct investigations into their lifestyles. The editorial department was thrown into chaos.

When Old Hep sauntered in through his front door that

evening, after abandoning the textile worker in the ruined factory, he was met by a flying thermos. Fortunately it struck his chest, not his head. Bowing his head in shame, he could see his wife's tie-dye skirt printed with pictures of ancient philosophers. (This garment was for export only – no one else in town had one like it.) As it approached him, he searched his mind for a way to handle the situation. But before he had time to reach a decision, a slender leg sheathed in a transparent nylon stocking (also imported) popped out from under the skirt and kicked him in the groin. Old Hep shrieked with pain, and cowered on the floor just like the textile worker had done a few hours earlier. The pain was excruciating. He saw a sea of gold stars dart before his eyes. The female novelist kicked him again and Old Hep's tired shoulders caved in. Then the novelist dragged him into the light, seated herself in her armchair, handed him his pink exercise book and told him to read from it the passages she had underlined in red pencil.

Everything that happened after that had vanished from his mind by the time he was lying in bed, apart from his tearful confession, and his wife's demand that he apologise officially to his work unit and submit himself to investigation. 'If you don't do as I say, I will take you to court,' she threatened before dozing off.

Now she was sleeping like a log, and Old Hep was lying awake beside her, miserably counting the hours until dawn. In the past the night had belonged to him, but now everything was finished and all that remained for him was fear. This fear coursed through his blood, then spread to his bones and nerve channels. He felt like the dead rat he had once seen lying on a cold street corner. It had lain there for three days. In his mind, he always connected the rat with a female colleague, because she had dared walk up to within a step of it and stand over it with her legs wide open. When she dragged him over to take a look, he shrieked with terror and felt as though his head were about to explode. It was the same fear he felt when the Red Guards dragged his father to their front door and pulled him into the baying crowds outside. He knew that in these moments of terror, he was naked and alone. The face of the rotting rat flashed once more before his eyes. The Red Guards were pushing him into a well of darkness, the tigress was baring her teeth, ready to devour him. No one was coming to his rescue. He and his father were surrounded. The voices of the crowd were so deafening that all he could hear was the rage thundering through his body. He knew that they – the crowd outside – were one great mass, and that he was on his own. For a moment, he could see his own eyes grafted onto the dead rat's face. They were dirty and motionless, but alive. They could see everything.

What he had appreciated most after he got married was the security of living under the tigress's benevolent protection. He could hide quietly behind her while she dealt with any problem that turned up. She was tall and sturdy, a wall he could lean against. Had she not been swept up by the Open Door Policy, permed her hair, glossed her lips and been included in *The Great Dictionary of Chinese Writers*, his life would still be worth living now. Her strict and inflexible attitude suited him well; he had grown accustomed to it. She was a mother to him and he enjoyed living under her wing. He had hoped that his life would continue like this for ever.

In the early hours of the morning, her breathing grew deeper and louder, and once again he was seized by the recurring terror of being swamped by a baying crowd. He sensed his wife seize his arm and shove him outside the door. Immediately he was surrounded by a hostile mob. There was nothing for him to grab hold of, he was alone and powerless. His eyes were open like his father's, like the dead rat's, but he couldn't see a thing.

An idea suddenly came to him. 'I must escape!' he muttered. 'Make sure they never catch me.' He thought about a divorcee he'd been seeing on the side. She lived on her own. Perhaps he could stay with her. Although she wore lipstick and painted her nails like his wife, and even read the same books as her, at least she didn't have a bad temper. Her main fault was that she always burst into tears after a couple of drinks. But lying in his bed, he could no longer remember her name. He thought of all the women listed in his 'Compendium of Beauties', but couldn't put names to any of them either. Then he thought about the textile worker, and how her lips had trembled with fear the first time he kissed her.

His thoughts were suddenly interrupted by a sense of impending doom. The feeling seemed as real as his daydreams. He turned round to look at the undulating tigress, and his body went cold. He realised that the dead rat was in fact himself.

Terrified that his wife might find out his true identity, he slipped under the bed. Everything seemed larger underneath. He wondered why the dead rat's eyes had been so wide open, and he hoped his own weren't open so wide. He crawled into the kitchen. From the ground, everything looked familiar, yet strange. He glimpsed parts of the kitchen he'd never seen before. Underneath the sink he found a large web with two spiders sleeping in the centre, locked in an embrace. Between two empty bottles he saw an old sprouting potato and a jar of mustard he thought he'd thrown away months ago. The sky outside the window was getting lighter. He tried to decide on a plan of action. The tigress would be waking up soon. He rose to his feet and set to work on making breakfast. When he realised he must first tackle the pile of dirty plates, he slipped into a daydream, as he always did before starting the washing-up.

He climbed into the control cabin of the steamship and grabbed hold of the wheel. But instead of letting the ship fly into the sky, he steered it down into the deep blue sea. A maintenance worker ran over and told him to stop. He said the ship had sprung a leak and was sinking fast. 'Why are you still steering?' the worker asked, glaring at him sternly.

A few months later, the professional writer saw the editor creeping through the corridors of the People's Cultural Centre. He seemed to move like a ball of dough that was being pulled by invisible hands. His wife had thrown him out of the flat, and he was spending his nights on a fold-up bed in the corner of his office. Without a woman to lean on, he had lost his bearings and developed all the characteristics of an old man. He had become dirty, slow-witted, forgetful. His body gave off an indefinable odour that made one's stomach turn. His fashionable clothes looked out of place on his now withered and hunched frame. At noon he would walk down to the Cultural Centre's forecourt to play chess with the old pensioners who gathered there. The writer was taken aback by his transformation. Looking at him then, no one would have believed that this grubby old man had served as editor of the town's most prestigious literary magazine for fourteen years.

The writer's mind turns to the female novelist, a woman he slept with once. Immediately he remembers the smell of make-up and tobacco on her face. He still bumps into her sometimes outside the Writers' Association or at some literary event, and is taken aback by her haggard appearance. It always amazes him how some women seem to turn old overnight. He holds her responsible for their moment of intimacy. One night two years ago, he went to her flat to offer advice on her latest novel. When he arrived, he found the lights were dimmed, there were candles burning, and Old Hep was out of town. He fell into her trap without resistance, but regretted it almost at once. He found her shallow, and resented what he saw as her undeserved literary success.

She had no imagination, he says to himself. She relied on her string of affairs to provide her with material for her tearful love stories. The critics claimed she was a great writer, they said her books were inspired. To achieve success as an author these days, you have to have led a troubled life. The more you have suffered, the better your books will sell. Today's women understand the importance of time, but ignore the need for direction. They focus on the colour of a lampshade, they worry about which parts of their bodies to cover or expose. As soon as they find a man to act as their safe shore, they start floating through life like a boat drifting aimlessly out to sea. She was a boat stranded in mid-ocean, and the editor (it sickens me even to think about the old man) was a dirty sock she had discarded years before but was still floating by her side.

Today, the editor is an old pensioner who walks through the

park every morning, listening to his portable radio. His wife divorced him last year and opened a hardware store in an empty room in the Writers' Association. This innocent-looking shop is in fact a front for a variety of black market activities. Through her father's military connections she is able to secure many sought-after licences and buy products that she can sell on for double the price. She has made a small fortune, and has lost interest in writing. Her business career is much more compatible with this crippled society, and it has given her the ultimate signs of success: a Western Dream mattress, wallpaper, electric kettle, a 28-inch television, a set of porcelain crockery, a jar of Nescafe, a bottle of French wine, aluminium window frames, and the centrally heated apartment that contains all these things.

'Is this what we all work for?' the professional writer asks out loud. 'What we go to university for, make friends for? Tell me, is it worth all the pain?'

'What pain?' The blood donor stubs his cigarette out. He has become almost as fond of asking questions as the writer.

'What I mean is – all literature has its cost. Writers must suffer for their art.' The professional writer doesn't want to pursue his previous train of thought.

'Everything has its cost. If you work hard enough, you can buy anything you want. Except time, of course,' the blood donor says, triumphantly.

'Yes, except time.' The writer knows that his fling with the female novelist was meaningless, there were no feelings involved. He admits that when she was a young woman, her writing had shown great promise, but it never lived up to expectations. All she produced in the end was a stream of inconsequential words. The professional writer smiles complacently, convincing himself that the reason he is unable to finish his novel is because he is practising self-control. However, in his heart he knows that he is even more worthless than the female novelist. He lacks the courage to commit himself to one thing entirely, or to jump into the thick of things. He wants to be a bystander, an objective witness, but in order to keep himself fed, he is forced to rely on others and submit himself to their needs.

He is lazy by nature, and self-obsessed, and is destined to eke out the rest of his life on the poverty-stricken margins of society. He will never settle down to any serious work. There is always some obscure detail to research or mundane duty to perform, and while these provide a welcome distraction, they also give him excuses to delay what he needs to do. However, these diversions pull him back to the real world. Without them, he would spend his entire life suspended in mid-air.

The lights have gone out once more, and the room is pitch black. For a moment, the professional writer feels like a plastic bag caught in the high wind. It occurs to him that although the plastic bag is worthless, it is able to rise above the mundane world and change directions. When the wind blows against it, it fills with air and glides through space – things the earth-bound can never do.

The Street Writer *or*
The Plastic Bag in the Air

In his mind, the professional writer sees the street writer squatting on a pavement in the new part of town, which a few years ago was open fields. It is a brand new district by the sea, built of concrete and cement. The local peasants who were evicted from their land and rehoused in the new three-storey concrete blocks are not yet accustomed to their new way of life. They still keep their timber and mouldy raincoats outside their front doors, even though they will never again have to burn wood or labour in the fields. The women continue to tie black scarves around their heads, although they no longer need to shield themselves from the sun. The men wear Western suits now, but still smoke their water pipes every afternoon. They always stand at an angle, as though they were leaning on their hoes in the fields. The children continue to shit in the streets rather than use the new toilets in their bathrooms. The flat roofs are pierced by a clutter of television aerials. Farmers from the hinterland who have found work in town but have failed to secure a residency permit, flock to this new district to rent private rooms. The local peasants have become wealthy landlords overnight, and the residents of the old town have been forced to take notice of the 'cabbage-faced bumpkins' they have previously preferred to ignore.

The street writer fixed his eyes on a plastic bag that was floating through the sky, and allowed all thoughts to empty from his mind. Passers-by assumed he was looking at the newly restored church, or the acacia tree beside it. No one could have guessed that he was staring at the plastic bag, or indeed that he was in fact squatting down for that sole purpose. In this dusty, drab corner of the street, he and the plastic bag became one.

He had come to this town on the spur of the moment, without even having applied for a residency transfer. The gloom and smog of his hometown depressed him, and besides, he couldn't afford to pay the compulsory three-hundred-yuan annual insurance fee that his metalwork factory now demanded from all employees. So he left his job and moved to this fast-developing town by the sea, which he then stuck to like a blob of chewing gum. After a while, the police got tired of arresting him for illegal residency and left him alone. He picked up a string of menial jobs. He washed dishes in a restaurant, worked as a security guard in a bar (although he wasn't even strong enough to fend off a cripple), he delivered canisters of butane gas, collected plastic bottles, and transported leftover restaurant slops to private pig farmers in the suburbs. After two years of hard toil, he set up business as a self-employed street writer. People paid him to write letters of complaint, business letters and shop signs. His only tools were a pen, some paper and a stack of envelopes.

He became familiar with the latest documents issued by the local Party committee and the major departments of central government. He learned about marriage procedures, finance and publication laws, business taxes, private enterprise regulations, landlords' rights, traffic laws, the latest developments in the policy of 'Redressing Past Injustices', and compensation for injuries at work. The complaints he wrote for his clients were coherent and well-argued, and conformed to the usual practice. He helped families condemned as rightists to gain rehabilitation, and victims of industrial injuries to secure financial compensation. Amorous young men paid him to write love letters to their girlfriends; wives of unfaithful artists paid him to write denunciations of their husbands that were to be read in the divorce courts; tenants and landlords paid him to fill out their tenancy contracts; illiterate peasants paid him to read out any letters they received. He carried out his tasks with great care, and his fees were reasonable. His speciality lay in the writing of love letters. If a client sent one of his letters to a woman, it was guaranteed that the next day she'd agree to sit next to him on a park bench.

If we pick out just one letter from the thousands he wrote, we will be able to see the fluidity of his style, his commitment to his art, and his deep insight into human nature. He dreamed of becoming a professional writer, or at least an intellectual. (Although he based the letters on what his clients asked him to write, he always refined the vocabulary and style, hitting the right note every time.) His words flowed in a continuous stream, like moonlight glittering on the surface of a river.

One day he wrote a letter for an old woman who was hoping to dissuade her daughter from pursuing a relationship with a professional writer. As the letter bore little relation to what she had asked for, she returned it to him the same afternoon and demanded a refund. The writing of this letter caused the street writer so much distress that he considered abandoning his profession. Here's an extract from the rejected letter:

. . . It's curiosity that first draws men and women together, not love. They are curious to know whether they could ever be united into one. Your father was a writer. He wrote articles for newspapers, but never managed to publish a book. I stumbled into a relationship with him without thinking things through. At first I was drawn to his unusually large face – it was the size of a plantain leaf. His gaze made me smile and blush. The day a woman's skin first feels the touch of a man's lips, she loses her fear of the breasts hidden beneath her clothes, and is happy for the man to touch them and squeeze them.

I was as curious about my anatomy as he was, and I let this man with the large face caress and fondle my entire body, then prise my legs apart. The act that followed was horrifically obscene. Had I known as a young girl that women must spend half their lives with their legs wide open, so that men may thrust themselves in between, I certainly would never have let myself get involved with them. When I first smiled at the plantain-leaf face, I never imagined that my blush was somehow connected to that vile organ of his. Before long, I had 'fallen in love', or at least that's what my friends told me. I assumed that 'love' referred to all those shameful, sordid feelings one experiences when a man takes possession of one's body. Once we had become familiar with one another's intimate parts, we were able to move in together, and my friends told me how blissfully compatible we were.

I was foolish. Even when I found out what this so-called 'love' amounted to, I failed to put a stop to it. On the contrary, I was happy to satisfy his every craving, and we became stuck to each other like glue. We would expend our energies, collapse in exhaustion, then have a meal and fall asleep. This was the pattern of our days, it was called 'normal married life'. Then you came along. The one good thing about your birth was that it destroyed our sex life. Today you are the age that I was when I first met him. If you listen to what your mother has to say, perhaps you will choose a better path for yourself.

My first piece of advice is: never believe anything a man tells you. Above all, never trust a writer – they trap you in a web of words from which there is no escape. They earn their living making things up, they are professional liars. They tell you stories about things that never happen in the real world. At least, I've never witnessed any love story like the ones they write about in their books.

I presume that you and the writer have commenced a sexual relationship, because if he has already spoken to you of love, he has no doubt been simultaneously making moves on your body. If this is the case, perhaps you have discovered that love is a word of little consequence that men spew from their mouths without thinking. Or perhaps your curiosity about sex has blinded you to love's true nature. We are both women. We are fully acquainted with the various mounds and dips of our bodies, and know they are not nearly as sublime as men imagine. You must fend men off for as long as possible, because as soon as they have squeezed and probed every part of your flesh, you become worthless to them, no better than a lump of meat on a chopping board. Don't wait for your wedding day before you start knocking some sense into him. Tell him at once that he must stop dragging you off to bed, or to deserted sheds and grassy verges. Ensure that you remain standing or seated at all times. Never give him an opportunity to press you down onto the floor.

You convince yourself that his search of your body is a search for love. But love cannot be groped or fondled . . .

He had based the ten-page letter on the information the old woman gave during their conversation. She said she had tried to write the letter herself, but her hands shook so much she was unable to hold a pen. The street writer was stunned by her candour and her cynical attitude to love.

When he remembered the cold expression on her face, his skin crawled. He blushed when he thought of the sentimental love letters he had written in the past. He knew that the women who had received them were now waddling contentedly down the street, clutching their pregnant bellies, while the men who had sent them were returning to him on the sly, asking him to pen letters to their new mistresses.

'Love is a waste of time,' the old woman told him. 'If that writer wants to marry my daughter, he should come and take a look at me first. I'm the image of who she will be nine thousand days from now. When he sees me, his love-sickness will vanish like a puff of smoke.'

The old woman mumbled on to him about how young people today confuse heartache with suffering. She said they are two different things: real suffering courses through the body like blood, but heartache is a fleeting reaction to a petty lovers' tiff. She said if one feels elated with the joys of love, then it means one has not delved fully enough into one's partner's soul. Finally, after she told him that the daughter who ignored all her letters was planning to perform a public suicide, she cried: 'She really is my reincarnation! Nobody can stand in her way. She's planning to hire a tiger from the zoo and feed herself to it. If she returns to this world, we'll form an unbeatable team.'

After the old woman walked away, the street writer had to tap his head before he could think clearly again. That evening, he returned to his shed in the entrance passage of an apartment block in the centre of town, and tried to sort out the old woman's muddled thoughts. (Apparently the shed's previous owners – a mother and son who ran a private crematorium business – had taken a trip to the suburbs one day, and hadn't been seen again since.) He focused his mind; the light bulb hanging above him shone on his balding head. Although he lacked the old woman's sharp eyes that could see through the vanity of this world, the grey matter inside his skull had been taxed so hard over the years that wiry hairs jutted from his nostrils.

He had a face that indicated he was not suited to manual labour. It was heart-shaped, and as white as the moon. His lips were as moist and red as those of a young girl – although this was probably an early sign of tuberculosis. The whites of his eyes were yellow. He often smiled for no reason. When he was listening to the old woman's story, and later writing the letter for her, the smile had never once left his face.

As he sat beneath the light bulb staring at the brick wall, his thoughts turned to Chi Hui, a girl he had been writing to for one of his clients. Although he developed strong feelings for almost every woman he wrote to, it was to Chi Hui that his mind returned most frequently. Thinking about her, he felt his spirit take flight like a plastic bag dancing in the wind. In the past, thoughts of her made him reflect on maple leaves in spring, the smell of foreign cigarettes, the similarity between urethras and the gutters on the streets, or a couple embracing casually as they emerge from the public latrines. But the old woman's words had upset his usual pattern of thought, and his mind became confused.

(In the late dusk, the professional writer often sees the street

116

writer stumbling across the intersection in the centre of town. It always strikes him that he has the eyes of an insecure youth, the balding head of a middle-aged man, the wrinkled brow of a sixty-year-old and the body of a child. He has no idea what's going through his mind, but he longs to find out. Perhaps this is why he always keeps an eye out for him on the streets.)

'The Absurd is more real than life itself,' the street writer scribbled on the corner of his newspaper.

The letters he composed revealed nothing of his true character. In each one, he adopted a different voice. He could take on the role of a lawyer, a schoolgirl, a peasant, or a widow. He could be anyone, no matter what age or gender. If one had to fix an identity to him, one would have to say he was a composite of all the roles he assumed. Each letter was a new beginning for him, an opportunity to try out a new persona. Sometimes he felt as though he were skating on ice, in random overlapping circles. He knew where he had started from, but had no idea where he was going.

In the morning, he lodged complaints on behalf of plaintiffs, in the afternoon he wrote rebuttals for the defendants. He would write passionate professions of love, but would often have to pen the rejection notes that followed. He couldn't help feeling sad for the people whose love he helped turn down. He lived his life through his letters. Late at night when all was quiet, the words he had written would churn inside him like grass in a cow's stomach. Among the piles of paper on his desk was the draft of a letter he had written the week before, which started: 'Dear Comrade Chi Hui, It's time we put an end to our relationship (although it saddens me deeply) . . .' The street writer remembered having to beg his client to allow him to add the phrase in brackets. He had written thirty-five love letters to Chi Hui for this client, and had experienced the anxiety of the first declaration of love, the steamy passion that ensued, opposition from the girl's father and work unit, the attempted transfer of residency permits, a brief affair with a third party, a weepy reconciliation, and now the final break-up. He was tortured by the thought of the pain he had caused Chi Hui. He felt a sudden urge to betray his feckless young client, and disclose to Chi Hui all the young man's hidden faults. What troubled him most was that the day after he wrote the final letter to Chi Hui, this fool asked him to write a letter to a new girl.

He turned the draft letter over, picked up his pen and wrote: 'I can see your sad little face, your raven-black hair blowing in the wind. There are tears in your eyes. How could he have broken up with you so cruelly? Do you realise that I helped him write that letter to you? You should see his handwriting – it's a disgrace! You have been in my thoughts all year. I have read every letter you sent back to him, my darling.' (Even though he wrote love letters for a living, a blush always rose to his face when he used terms of affection like this.)

Turning the page over again, he read: 'You mean nothing to me now. You only chose to go out with me because Yuci had dumped you. I just filled the gap. Yuci showed me the letters you wrote him. They were much more loving than the ones you sent me.' Then, in his own note to Chi Hui he wrote: 'I wrote that letter myself, word for word. Chi Hui, I can't bear to think of you reading it. I'm terrified that you might get hold of some sleeping pills. If only I could fly to you twice as fast as that damn letter to stop it contaminating your hands.'

Flicking to the other side again, he read: 'You depress me. And so does your dull family. I feel like a corpse when I'm with you. Your graceful exterior cannot hide the ugly scars left by your terrorised childhood.'

'I love your charming gestures, Chi Hui,' he continued on the other side (even though he had never seen this girl who lived a thousand kilometres away). 'I love your family, I love your frailty. Your background and character happen to match mine exactly.' He paused for a moment, overcome by a momentary sense of pride, then continued: 'Of all the young ladies I've seen . . .' (his clients sometimes showed him photographs of their loved ones) 'you are the most beautiful. You have the melancholy air that is characteristic of our classical "fragile beauties". We are both thin and weak. We should spend our lives together in sickness, tending to one another's needs. When I look at you, I see the first snow of winter falling on my home town, the frosted windows of a wooden cabin, a cup of steaming milk tea. Oh, I can't forgive myself for writing those cruel letters to you!' On the other side, he had berated her gourd-shaped face and lifeless expression. 'I have corresponded with you for a whole year. How can I just abandon you now in such a heartless way? I must be mad!'

He turned the sheet back and forth. He knew both sides of it were real, and that he was trapped in between. He was aware that he'd made some progress, though. Ten years ago, he was a feeble young man who was prone to tears and could only digest minute quantities of food. Now, however, he was a mature man of thirty with a range of complex emotions. As a boy, he only liked to watch sad films. When he saw the heroine die in the Korean film *The Flower Girl,* he cried in front of his classmates. He was always drawn to people with scars on their bodies, because he knew that each scar represented a moment of pain.

He continued his note to Chi Hui: 'I longed to have a scar as a child, but I was sixteen before I finally succeeded in cutting myself. My inertia and lethargy have prevented me from achieving anything of great importance in life. Perhaps my poor digestion and weak heart are to blame. I chose to become a street writer because I thought it would cure me of my loneliness, but now I find myself vexed by a multitude of worries. These anxieties are bad for my health. Whether I see parents saying goodbye to their children at a train station, or a group of friends chatting and laughing, I always feel a wave of nausea.'

After a brief hesitation, he went on: 'I often feel I'm so light that I could drift into the sky. To prevent this happening, I keep lumps of metal in my pockets to weigh me down. Sometimes, my feet seem to leave the ground. I'm so small and thin, I wonder why the wind hasn't carried me away yet.' He stopped again, sensing that he was now just writing to himself. He knew that in the end, he always managed to disappear from the page. He could be whatever people needed him to be, but he was never able to enter their lives.

As the street writer sits under the lamplight, we can examine his haggard face and slowly vanishing body. (In his notes, the professional writer often remarks on the street writer's smile and premature wrinkles. Anyone who has grown up in a fishing village will immediately picture the street writer as a shrimp that has just been scooped from the sea.) His frail and sickly appearance allowed him to melt into the background, but it didn't stop his business from flourishing. His skills were in great demand. Illiterate migrants who settled in the town's new district were grateful for his service, as it enabled them to pass themselves off as locals. Young people who had left school early also relied on him to fill the gaps in their education. They milled around him all day. He would smile knowingly as they passed on to him all the latest gossip about their neighbours. He received information faster than the speed of a telegram, and was the first person people turned to if they wanted to know what had happened that day.

'Have you seen that cat again?' people asked as they passed him on the street corner. His knowledge concerning the notorious 'foreign cat incident' had made him famous throughout the town. A foreign cat the size of a dog had escaped from a chemical plant run by a Sino-Western joint venture. The plant's delivery driver, Old Sun, was one of the first to hear about the escape. Since he knew that the cat often scurried past the street writer, Old Sun asked him if he'd seen it recently. The street writer then divulged all the information he had picked up about the case. He told him that because the foreign cat had one blue eye and one red eye, and could say 'Good-bye', 'Good morning', 'Long live Chairman Mao' and 'Pig' in English, it was arrested, interrogated, and detained on charges of foreign espionage. The police discovered a bugging device and telegraph transmitter fixed to its tail, and behind its eye a miniature camera that had been secretly photographing the dark side of China's socialist system. The curious thing, though, was that during its interrogation by two officials from the National Security Department, it cried out 'Long live Chairman Mao.' The reactionary spy was clearly trying to pull the wool over their eyes. The night they were preparing to escort the cat to Beijing, it bit through its chains and escaped. The street writer said he had seen it several times, scampering past him then disappearing over the high wall across the road. It was a year later before the police officers finally tracked the cat down and beat it to death with wooden sticks.

The street writer would work late into the night, classifying the drafts he had written during the day, and attaching notes to them. The notes might remind him to ask the client for details of their family background and political status, in case the police decided to check his records. In the new urban district that resembled a plaster stuck over an old wound, he had become acquainted with many important people, including the director of the Party committee of the Industrial and Commercial Management Department, and a poultry farmer who had been selected as the local representative to the National People's Congress. The illiterate farmer received sackloads of letters exposing various crimes and cases of official corruption, as well as applications for residency transfers. The poor delegate could be seen every day, tramping up and down the streets on his way to discuss one of the multitude of disputes he had been called upon to solve. His suit grew dirtier and his back more bent by the day. Children walking home from school would trail behind him and chant:

> *Little old man with a crooked back*
> *Falls in a dung pit and picks up a cowpat . . .*

If he was not sleeping or writing letters for his clients, the street writer's mind would always turn to the draft love letters piled on his desk. To him, they were the most precious things in his life. They contained descriptions of his loved ones, declarations of passion sprinkled with a few obscene words that, since the Open Door Policy, no longer condemned one to a life in prison – words like 'love', 'soft lips', 'the sun around which I revolve' and 'melancholy'. He felt affection for every woman he wrote to, he poured his heart out to them. He kept not only the drafts of the letters he sent them, but also the letters they sent back to his clients. He developed a deep understanding of female emotions, and treasured the insight he gained into women's most intimate thoughts.

On summer evenings, when couples were strolling outside in the warm sea breeze, the street writer would lean over his desk, hard at work, the sweat pouring from his brow. The tasks his clients assigned him never fully satisfied his creative desires. In his bones he was a poet. When people fell in love in spring, as they invariably did, he employed all his poetic skills to fall in love on their behalf. When autumn drew in, he would write letters breaking off the affairs. If there were a thousand love letters in spring, he would have to write over nine hundred rejection letters in autumn. His life was very much tied to the seasons.

His complicated love life made him nervous, and when he returned to his shed each day, he would check every corner of the room to see whether someone was hiding there. The search took nearly half an hour to complete, because the previous owner had crammed the corners with planks of wood that he had planned to make furniture with. There were also six or seven boxes filled with burial clothes, paper lanterns and incense coils, and under the bed that took up a third of the room was another heap of odds and ends. When he lay on the bed at night, he always worried about what was hidden below, and whether someone had sneaked underneath to spy on him. Before entering the shed, he would stick his ear to the front door and listen for any noises. He kept a hammer under his pillow so that he could deal with anything that might appear at the foot of his bed at night. He made marks on the wooden boxes, and checked them regularly to ensure that nothing had been moved. In a secret drawer of his wardrobe, he hid the letters he wrote to his clients' women in which he expressed to them his undying love. Of course, he never posted them. They were the most personal and truthful letters he ever wrote.

As time went by, he became increasingly anxious about the content of these secret letters. Sometimes he would sneak one out from the bottom drawer and cross out a few lines before returning it carefully to its place. From a letter he wrote to Chi Hui, he erased the line: 'Oh life, you move too fast. Take my hand, and stay for a while, and tell me what you're all about.' A scrap of paper he tore from another letter and consigned to the bin was marked with the words: 'This ink pen has written letters to you for seven years. It understands me, forgives me. You can ask it any question you like, if you harbour any doubts about my love for you.' Another rejected passage read: 'Women hold an irresistible attraction for me. With one of you by my side, I feel warm and at peace. You radiate waves that seep into every part of my body. Whether I am sitting on the corner of the street or in the back of a cinema, just one glimpse of the downy hairs on your skin sends me into a rapture.'

He stared at the long shadow on the wall above the chest in the corner of the room. 'It really does look like a policeman tonight,' he told himself. He had often thought of clearing the shed of all its clutter, including the planks of wood, but he was never at home during the day, and he was afraid that at night the noise would draw the attention of the neighbours and police.

One morning, however, he decided to stay in and give his room a thorough clean. He tore down the red cloth that hung along the centre of the bed and put it away in the chest. He then gave the table and walls a lick of paint, and decorated the room with new calendars printed with pictures of auspicious red-crowned cranes and photographs of the film star Liu Xiaoqing. When he lay in bed that evening, the room seemed much more welcoming. That night he slept so well, he ejaculated in his dreams.

At three or four in the morning, he was woken by a soft, muffled noise. He opened his eyes and saw a long, thin shadow flitting around the room.

'Who's there?' he asked, beads of sweat dripping from his furrowed brow. Now he could see the shadow was an old hag with long white hair and ingot-shaped shoes.

'That incinerator was too hot,' the shadow said, humming

123

like a mosquito. 'I'm looking for a piece of cloth that hasn't faded yet.' She bent down and rummaged inside the chest.

'This is my home!' he replied, breaking into a sweat.

The flickering apparition laughed. 'Ha! But I have lived here all my life! I know every corner of this room like the back of my hand. When the dirty handkerchief under your pillow was new, I used to keep my ring inside it. Have you taken a look under the bed yet?'

The street writer shook his head from side to side, and discovered he was still alive, and that the old hag flitting before his eyes was alive too. The strands of black hair on his balding head stood up on end. He opened his mouth, his tongue thirsting for a drop of water.

'What's under the bed?' he asked. He watched the old hag move towards him, then lower herself, or rather fall, onto the bed. 'What a pathetic creature you are,' she hummed. 'You're as thin as a matchstick. How much longer are you planning to stay here?'

'But I live here,' he said to the dim and blurry face. These words soothed his nerves, and soon the hairs on his head drooped back down onto his scalp. He suspected that he was speaking to a ghost. This was a regular occurrence for him. He had been visited by the ghosts of the Virgin Mary and Chairman Mao, a girl he had seen in a magazine, and a woman with small feet who had walked past him on the street. One night, when the spirit of a policeman who had harassed him a few years previously paid a visit, he slapped his face and knocked his helmet off. Who knows, maybe this muddle-headed old woman was just another of those ghosts. He attempted to get out of bed, just as he'd done when he went to slap the policeman, but his legs couldn't stop shaking.

'You little worm,' the old hag said, in the same harsh tone she used with her son. 'You're like a maggot burrowing into a corpse. You run into our shed every night, pretending to be mad, always calling out some woman's name. In a few thousand days, those girls will be like the old housewives you see outside, dragging their children down the street. Even the freshest face will one day resemble a chunk of salted gammon. All women become smelly and clumsy in middle age. Why didn't you listen to what the mother of that actress told you? Why are you still here, wasting your time writing those obscene letters?'

As the old hag sank to the floor, he heard a rustling noise from inside the chest. Two mice scuttled out from under the bed and jumped into the lowest drawer of his desk.

'Why not put an end to it now? You'll have to go sooner or later, so you might as well get it over with. Ha! I see our belongings are still here. At least you haven't stolen anything.' The rustling noise came to a stop. He put his hand over his lungs and heart to check whether he was still alive. When all the sounds died down, he sat up in his bed, turned the light on and waited for dawn to break.

Early next morning, he returned to his corner of the street. It was a fine day. He could tell there was no wind because the plastic bag wasn't moving and the white clouds in the sky were perfectly still. Squatting down against the wall, he hunched his shoulders and wondered why his spirits were so low. Perhaps he was upset by the old hag who had pestered him last night, or by what the mother of the actress had told him the week before, or perhaps the strain of writing so many letters every day was finally taking its toll. Having lived away from his family so long, his thoughts often drifted back to his hometown, although the sight of the white plastic bag always flicked him back to the present as fast as the snap of a rubber band. Now, as he squatted in the corner, he remembered how, as a child, when the maple leaves were turning red, he had walked up to a tree, his eyes brimming with tears, pulled out a pencil and carved into the trunk the words 'Help me! Help me!' Even from an early age, he liked to write down words to express what was on his mind. He remembered standing for hours in front of a shop counter gazing at the fountain pens he couldn't afford to buy; running all day along the banks of a river after his mother had slapped him in front of his classmates; secretly grieving for a girl next door who had committed suicide; pulling out the first shoots of grass in spring and rolling naked over the bare earth.

Now, as a man of thirty, he felt that the hopes that each new spring had promised were empty and deceitful. He had discovered that the stages of his life's journey were in fact as neatly mapped out as the Chinese characters on the pages of his draft letters. He knew he presented a pitiful sight, and that his mind was filled with dry and meaningless memories. The old hag who had badgered him last night was right – he was a piece of scum, stuck by gob to the street corner.

He picked up his pen. Whatever happened, he knew he had to write. Two peasants who had asked him to draw up a complaint were standing patiently by his side. They had travelled into town to report that their village Party secretary had murdered a widow and her children. After the street writer finished the letter, he helped them post it and invited them for a meal. When the peasants looked up at him gratefully from the restaurant table and squeezed the white dumplings in their trembling black hands, thoughts filled his mind once more. He had seen many peasants like them before, on the trains he took back to his hometown. They lived like cockroaches, scuttling from one place to the next, struggling to make a living. He thought of how, when they sat in the trains, the smells of rancid food wafting from their fake leather bags would merge with the stench from the toilets at the end of the carriage.

Whenever he returned home, he felt as frail and vulnerable as a silkworm that had just shed its cocoon. His residency permit would forever be fixed to his place of birth; he had no backdoor connections to help him apply for a transfer. The only way he could survive in this coastal town was to melt into the background. He seldom entered shops, and only visited the public showers once a month, making sure to sneak in just before closing time. He only dared fetch water from his outside tap in the middle of the night. To avoid washing his clothes and then having to hang them out to dry, he just scraped the oil and dirt from shirt collars every four days with the blade of his letter knife. He took his meals at one dumpling stall whose owner he trusted. He always left his shed early in the morning, before any of his neighbours were up. He was amazed he had managed to survive all these years without raising any serious alarms.

'Look at her make-up! She looks like a painted eggshell!' he mumbled, staring at a woman passing by on the street. He was shocked by this comment. He buried his head in his hands, grabbed a piece of paper and scribbled: 'I really have gone mad this time. Nothing seems real.' As the nib of his pen scratched across the page, the image of himself as a child flashed through his mind again. He saw himself aged six, climbing out of a box, looking up with large moist eyes and crying, 'Let go of me! I can get out by myself.' He grabbed the child and placed him down on the ground. The boy crawled across the floor, and suddenly one of his legs fell off. Then his head fell off, and rolled towards the beam of light slanting through the window. 'You're not real,' he said, walking over to the child and digging out the eyes from his face. He then saw the child's eyes displayed in a shop window. A fat woman bought the eyes and walked off with them, and he chased after her through a maze of narrow streets. It was a dream that had recurred for thirteen years.

'Those eyes see everything,' he often sighed, when he woke up from this dream. 'When I rise into the sky, I will fly like a bird.'

Walking home at night in the lamplight, he often saw the dismembered child falling to the ground like a feather. But tonight, as he approached the intersection in the centre of town, the old hag's words still racing through his mind, his thoughts cleared, and a terrible sense of guilt descended upon him. He felt ashamed of his dishonest profession, and all the love he had helped destroy. He had wanted to lead an honest life, but there was no place for honesty in this town.

In the silent hours before dawn, he was still awake, writing at his desk.

'Only through suffering can man gain wisdom. People who have never suffered are incapable of growing up. Happiness is a wooden cabin one finds after a long and difficult journey; people who take the easy path never get to see it. The unhappiness I've suffered in the past has been other people's unhappiness. It has left no mark on me.'

When the rake-thin street writer saw the truth at last he laughed out loud. He thought about what the mother of the actress had told him, and about the hundreds of love letters he had written. Although his clients had exploited his creative skills, they had supplied him with a great deal of knowledge. The women's intimate revelations had allowed the virginal street writer to mature gracefully. He realised that he had finally overcome his shyness and embarrassment, and that it was now time for him to seek out his own love. Stunned by this idea, he jumped onto his bed and stood still for a moment. He was elated. He would never have believed that the day might come for him to embark on a real love affair of his own.

'But whom shall I love?' he asked himself. Blushing, he thought of Chi Hui, the young woman from a distant province to whom he had written passionate love letters for an entire year. A fortnight ago, he had been ready to strangle his client for all the pain he had caused her. The love that had fallen from her letters like snowflakes had made him dizzy with confusion.

He pushed the cynical words of the actress's mother to the back of his mind, sat down on the ground and leafed through all the correspondence relating to Chi Hui. A strange passion welled up in his heart. He wanted to conduct a love affair with a woman all by himself. He wanted to suffer the agonies of love. He wanted to kiss someone, conquer them, adore them. He wanted a woman of flesh and bone. A thin layer of sweat moistened his face. He laughed with delight as he looked through the drafts of the letters he had sent Chi Hui. He realised he loved her, that perhaps he had always loved her. In these letters, he had written descriptions of her beautiful hair, teeth, dimples and breasts, and between each word and every line he had left traces of his love.

He rose to his feet and walked to his desk. An immense joy seemed to fill the room. The hitherto numb nerve endings in his groin and thighs suddenly came alive. His mind clouded, his chest ached with anticipation, his pulse quickened a beat. He imagined smiling coyly as Chi Hui shook her head at him. He scooped a pile of Chi Hui's letters into his arms and jumped back onto the bed. He ran his tongue over his upper lip, stretched one leg in front of the other and chuckled contentedly.

Hearing a soft knock at the door, he quickly swallowed his laugh. Experience had taught him that the sound of laughter always attracted the police. He fastened his belt, and like a man who has been summoned for interrogation, opened the door with his head hung low. A figure, smelling both stale and sweet, darted inside, slammed the door and stood in front of him. Through his eyelashes, the street writer recognised the face of the actress's mother. She twisted her large mouth into a smile, and gazed at him with eyes that were as deep and narrow as the eyes of a leopard.

'It's you . . .' he whispered, terrified and confused.

'My daughter committed suicide last night. She never listened to my advice.' The old woman edged closer and wrapped her arms around him.

He had no time to put up a struggle. The old woman carried the frail, tubercular street writer to the bed, and pressed her wine-stained lips over his mouth. The next image that shot through his mind was not Chi Hui and her flowing locks, or the policeman who had harassed him on the street corner – it was the old woman's dark eyes glinting in the lamplight. Then his mind went blank and all he could see was a white plastic bag floating in the still air. Suddenly, he felt his tiny body, like a puff of breath, plunge into a dark vat of grease. He tried to free himself from the old woman's grip, but before he could summon the energy, the lights went out, everything went black, and he could no longer see a thing.

Let the Mirror Be the Judge *or* Naked

The professional writer sees the girl running naked down the street, her drooping nipples as sad and lonely as the eyes of a blind man. In his mind, he still confuses this girl with the entrepreneur's mother, whose personality seems to have seeped into many of the characters of his unwritten novel.

The girl's breasts were large, plump, heavy, soft and pendulous. Women see these fleshy protrusions as tools for flirtation and nurture; for men, they are the inspiration for a multitude of criminal thoughts. Erudite students refer to them as bosoms; artists portray them as pink-tipped peaches; peasants merely regard them as objects that droop to the stomach and are grabbed hold of when babies need a feed. In the villages, men get to see naked breasts all the time; for them a bare breast is as unremarkable as a bare arm. But as soon as these protrusions enter the towns, they become objects of immense value. Modern women mystify them, hiding them inside tight brassieres. Photographers are always careful when they aim their cameras at a woman's chest, because they know that too much cleavage can lay them open to accusations of 'Bourgeois Liberalism', and consign them to a four-year stint in prison.

The more daring contemporary writers refer to them variously as 'curvaceous pillows', 'tender dumplings', 'rose petals', 'ripe grapes' and 'my longed-for refuge'. When describing the experience of touching a breast for the first time, they claim they 'joined the immortals', 'fainted with delight', 'tottered on the precipice between life and death'. As a reaction against this sentimentality, avant-garde writers prefer to use words like 'tits', 'knockers' and 'withered strawberries'.

With the advent of the Open Door Policy, a few facts about breasts have entered the public consciousness:

Large, round breasts signify a virtuous wife and able mother. Good marrying material.

Medium-sized, pert breasts with pale pink nipples signify the ideal mistress. (Breasts like these make artists drool with desire.)

Wobbly or drooping breasts, whether large or small, indicate a woman who has indulged excessively in sensual pleasures, and is past her prime.

Women with very small breasts are usually chaste and demure, and tend to be highly intelligent. Their lack of self-esteem produces a particular sensitivity, and they often show a talent for poetry or academic work. When attempting to seduce a man, they drape themselves in loose garments, turn the lights down and whisper sweet words into his ear. They gaze up at him affectionately, and try to divert his eyes away from their chest to their shapely legs, full lips, soft hands, flowing hair, or gracefully arched eyebrows. They secretly buy themselves breast pumps – a product available on the market since the Open Door Policy – and as soon as they return home, they bolt their doors and start pumping. A local department store received two thousand pumps one day, and sold out in under two hours.

A Japanese businessman investigated the Chinese breast market and decided to open the town's first cosmetic surgery. Women were offered injections of fluid that swelled the breasts for three days. During this time, their boyfriends could fondle and squeeze them without causing any pain. These injections were ideal for women who were approaching their wedding night, or a date which promised a night of passion. The clinic was also able to heighten flat noses, cut creases into hooded eyelids, smooth out wrinkles, pluck bushy eyebrows into elegant thin lines, or remove the eyebrows completely and replace them with tattooed arches. If you were unhappy with the size of your chin, width of your forehead, shape of your teeth or mouth, they could help you put them right too.

A few months later, the papers reported news of a great advance in scientific discovery. Following a hundred days of experiments, Chinese scientists had successfully produced a breast-enlarging cream. One technician carelessly smeared some of the product over her mouth during the tests, and a few minutes later her lips swelled to double their previous size. The manufacturers claimed that if a flat-chested woman rubbed two jars of the cream onto her chest, she would develop breasts the size of small dumplings. The papers also mentioned that foreign scientists had created a breast-enlarging technique that entails stuffing sacs of sticky translucent fluid inside the skin above the ribcage.

It seems that breasts play a very important part in our lives.

The young woman who had recently been assigned to the town's Cultural Propaganda Department owned the type of breasts that signify a good wife and able mother. When she was at university, the sight of her breasts caused male students to walk straight into the trees and lampposts by the side of the road. When she entered the cafeteria, the male students dropped their chopsticks, overcome with lust and awe. She realised that she was one in a thousand, the owner of two priceless treasures. But she also knew that she would have to spend the rest of her life worrying about when to hide them and when to show them off. She could close her eyes and be able to guarantee that her figure was more attractive and shapely than that of any of the girls surrounding her.

She had not always been so proud of her breasts. When the two lumps of flesh started protruding from her chest, she assumed she had contracted some disease, and was too afraid to tell her mother. When she understood that she was in fact becoming a woman, she felt guilty and ashamed. She sensed the eyes of the crowd focus on the breasts that stuck out so visibly from her tight shirt and wobbled from side to side as she walked down the street. She found it hard to get used to the scrutiny of the crowd, and spent her early teenage years with her shoulders hunched.

133

Women with pretty faces but flat chests know the importance of flicking their hair back flirtatiously. Some even learn to wiggle their bottoms when they walk past a man, expose some thigh when crossing their legs, or whisper suggestive words between their pink lacquered lips. Women who are neither pretty nor buxom have to rely on their intelligence, wide reading and refined manners if they want to arouse a man's desire. But before she had even left university, this girl was already aware that her soft, pale breasts were destined to be the overriding reason for men's interest in her, and the source of her future happiness. Having felt ashamed of them in the past, she now regarded them as mysterious and fascinating objects.

After she graduated from university, she moved to this town and took up the job assigned to her by the Party. She was to spend every day in an office with the same four women and one man. Had she not suffered the problems she encountered during her first month, she could have retained her post until she was sixty-two years old, then retired peacefully. It was a secure job. The first day she arrived in the office, the two cactus plants that had been hovering between life and death suddenly burst into a blaze of white flowers. The atmosphere immediately relaxed. She knew she was brimming with youth, and that each breath she exhaled filled the air with the scent of spring. Although her female colleagues felt secretly threatened by her arrival, they gave her a courteous welcome. But as soon as she left the room, they would start discussing whether her pale complexion was the result of an application of the imported 'Snowflake' cream, or whether her seemingly slender waist was in fact held in by a corset.

'Her stomach looked a little wobbly,' the elderly book-keeper informed the others after following the girl into the women's toilets.

The middle-aged translator looked up from her typewriter. 'Her face is so plump she has dimples in her cheeks already,' she said. 'When I turned forty, the skin on my face was still tight and smooth.'

'Not yet twenty years old, and she's already got the breasts of a matron,' Chairwoman Fan, the fifty-five-year-old virgin smirked. 'I wouldn't be surprised if she's had an abortion.'

The young secretary who had recently married joined in and said, 'Maybe she's injected them with something.'

'It looks to me like she's been rubbing them with cream,' the old virgin opined, returning to her seat by the window. 'Or else, she's let too many men squeeze them. Why else would they be so big?' If you had been observing Chairwoman Fan closely, you would have noticed a malicious spark in her eyes. She had worked at her desk by the window in the corner of the room for the last thirty years. Before the girl with big breasts arrived in the office, she had never bothered to engage in idle chatter with her colleagues. No one ever dared approach her desk, or even so much as glance out of her side of the window. She always ensured that the half of the window that her desk touched was kept immaculately clean. She stuck a 'No Smoking' sign over the top pane, and hung a length of cloth over the two lower panes to block out the sun's rays that hit her desk in the afternoon. Her corner of the room always smelt of wet galoshes and moth balls. The girl with big breasts was assigned the desk opposite her. From the old virgin's vantage point, the girl's bosoms did indeed look extraordinarily large. They protruded so far, they seemed as though they were about to attack the desk.

When the girl walked back from the toilets and returned to her chair, the four other women fell silent. They savoured this moment of secret complicity – they felt united by their shared opinion concerning the new girl's unusually large breasts. After that, when the girl strode into the office every morning, her eyes full of the joys of spring, the other women would assume fixed grins and exchange knowing looks.

Before she had received her first month's pay cheque, the girl had already made friends with the secretary, who was the youngest of her four female colleagues. The secretary revealed stories of her husband's violent temper in exchange for the girl's descriptions of university love affairs; she offered her a piece of nougat her husband had brought back from a business trip, and the girl gave her a plastic key-ring. Soon they started making jokes about the older colleagues, and were even on the point of sharing secrets about their friends' private lives.

The atmosphere in the office became strained. After the secretary broke ranks with the three older women, a cold war set in and the solidarity among the 'old guard' collapsed. If someone happened to bang a cup on the desk, a minute later, another colleague would slam a cup down more loudly. One morning, the translator walked in wearing a new flowery dress and announced that her chickens had stopped laying eggs and were only fit for the chopping board. Knowing that this was a veiled joke at her expense, the old virgin glanced at the translator and sneered, 'Did your daughter buy you that dress? It really takes years off you.' Their battles rolled over into the political study sessions. When the elderly book-keeper finished reading out a report about a local hero who had tragically drowned trying to save the life of a state-owned pig, the translator and the secretary appeared unmoved. They didn't even attempt a show of grief. Chairwoman Fan noticed their behaviour, and made a record of it in her notebook.

'They seem to have something against me,' the girl told the secretary one day after work. By this time, they were already so close that they were sharing snacks at lunchtime. Relations in the office had entered the stage of 'second-degree combat preparations'. Although one of the cactus plants was still blooming, the other had lost its flowers, and its needles had turned red and hard.

They walked towards the bus stop. For the last two days, they had taken to holding hands when walking outside together. The secretary led the way, and the girl allowed herself to be led. Every woman needs this kind of relationship. The secretary appreciated the intimacy, it compensated for all the domestic misery she had suffered since her wedding day. She enjoyed revealing the secrets of the bedroom to the girl who hadn't commenced sexual relations (or 'jumped into the sea', as the new saying went). In return, she experienced pleasures she had never enjoyed before: the sensation of the girl's innocent, warm hand in hers; the feeling of pity, similar to the pity a cat might feel before it strikes its prey; the knowledge that she had the power to control what might, or might not, happen to the girl. Her life suddenly seemed more interesting. She had tried to hold herself back time and again, but now she could contain herself no longer and she revealed at last the secret that she shared with her colleagues. 'They have fallen out with each other because of you,' she said.

'What?' The girl drew in a sharp breath of air. 'Why?'

The secretary didn't want to jeopardise her friendship with the girl. So, keeping the girl's hand firmly in her grip, she said in a comforting tone, 'Haven't you noticed what's been going on?'

The girl with big breasts had no idea what the secretary was talking about.

'Tell me what you know,' she cried. 'Tell me now!'

'Try and guess first.'

'Don't play games.' The girl's face turned red.

'It seems Chairwoman Fan was right.' The secretary was deliberately dragging things out.

'Please, sister, I beg you. Tell me.' The girl shrank back into the role of someone who needs to be protected.

This wasn't the first time the secretary had been called 'sister', so her expression didn't change. 'She's jealous of you – that stupid old hen who can't lay any more eggs.'

'What did she say about me?' The girl's face turned from red to white.

'It's your breasts,' the secretary said, touching the girl's arm softly. 'It's because you have such large breasts.' She was now using the tone of voice women adopt when speaking about contraception and sexual matters.

The girl covered her face with her hands and stopped in her tracks. The sense of inferiority that she had buried years before suddenly welled up inside her and dragged her back to the times when she would walk through the crowd hunching her shoulders like an old woman, the two lumps of flesh on her chest filling her with shame and fear. She remembered the time her mother humiliated her in front of her classmates, saying,

'You should be ashamed of yourself wearing that T-shirt. Everyone can see your nipples!' That night, she borrowed her mother's white bra and clamped her breasts to her chest. When she left her home the next day, she sensed that everyone knew that she was a girl with bound breasts.

The self-confidence she had worked so hard to achieve was now crumbling into pieces.

'What did they say?' The girl's faint voice was almost drowned by the loud footsteps on the pedestrian flyover above. The secretary hadn't expected the girl to be as embarrassed as this. She felt as though she were watching a lamb drowning in water, a lamb she could save with less energy than it would take to blow away a grain of dust. As a married woman, she knew many things the girl didn't know, but longed to know. Yesterday, she had told the girl about the pleasure of feeling a man's tongue run down her stomach. When she had brought up the subject of the girl's breasts a few moments ago, she had felt a dampness seep from between her thighs.

The secretary ventured a further question. 'Did you rub foreign creams on them, or inject them with something?' She gazed enviously at the girl's youthful complexion. It was as rosy as hers was before she married. She could sense how uncomfortable the girl was, and how fast her heart was beating.

In just a few seconds, the girl seemed to age ten years, her entire body appeared to shrink inwards. 'Never, never,' she protested. 'I have never had any injections, or used any foreign cream.'

'That's what I guessed,' the young woman continued. 'Perhaps Chairwoman Fan was right then.'

'What did she say?' For the first time in her life the girl was forced to discuss her breasts in public.

'That old virgin's a sly one,' the secretary said, glancing behind her to check that no one was listening. They had almost reached the bus stop. 'She said you've made them bigger by letting men fondle them. Actually, that's what I thought too, at first.'

The girl's face turned red again.

'Surely someone must have told you!' the secretary laughed. 'The more men fondle them, the bigger they get.'

'I've never let any man fondle them!' The girl's throat went dry. 'They've always been this big, ever since I was fourteen.' Her blush was spreading to her ears and neck now.

'There's nothing to be embarrassed about.' Although the secretary sympathised with her new friend, she still examined the girl's face, searching for the truth.

'But it's true!' The girl's head dropped in despair. She longed to extricate herself from this humiliating situation. 'You still don't believe me, do you?'

Without looking at one another, they quickened their pace, and the tenderness that had been established between them over the last weeks melted away. When they reached the bus stop, the girl joined the queue inside the barricade, while the secretary stood outside. During the previous few days, the secretary had always waited for the girl to catch her bus before continuing her walk home.

'Don't take it so seriously! So what if they talk about you? They're just jealous because they're so flat-chested.' Although the secretary's breasts drooped a little, she still qualified as a 'woman with breasts'.

'I've never had injections or taken pills.' A deep wrinkle wormed down the girl's smooth forehead.

'Times have changed. Those old matrons have been left behind. They're jealous of you, that's all. You're only twenty. So what if you've let some boy squeeze them bigger?' The secretary cast her eyes over the girl's ample bosoms. She could guess that they had incited many illicit events. Looking at them brought to mind episodes in her past, and the pleasure she felt when her husband squeezed her own breasts. 'As soon as men get near us, they want a feel. But I only let my husband suck mine before we go to sleep.' The secretary couldn't help revealing a few more details of her private life. Noticing that the girl was still frowning, she glanced towards the direction from which the bus was due to arrive, and swore at it for taking so long.

'Why do they have to talk about me?' The girl's voice was still faint. Nothing the secretary said could console her now. 'I was born this way,' she muttered quietly.

The secretary smiled at her and said: 'Don't take any notice of them. Those women are past their prime. I understand you. I wouldn't be shocked if you told me you were wearing a padded bra. There's nothing wrong with big breasts. Those women would still be flat-chested even if they wore ten padded bras.'

'I've never worn a padded bra in my life,' the girl sobbed.

The young woman didn't believe her for a second. 'You don't want them to be too big though, people will notice. Big-breasted women like us don't need to wear padded bras.'

The bus finally arrived, and the girl was carried aboard by the surging crowd. She felt as though her throat were stuffed with cotton wool. She carried her two heavy breasts back home and as soon as she opened her front door, ran to her bed and burst into tears.

'Let the mirror be the judge,' she whispered to herself as she stood in front of the rectangular mirror. For the first time in her life, she stared at length at the two large globes of plump flesh, each one crowned with a dried strawberry. The truth was, no man had ever placed his hands on them. At fourteen, when they first started to grow, they had caused her some pain. At university, they gave her a sense of pride. When she walked down the street and they shook up and down, they both annoyed and pleased her. From books she discovered that her type of breasts signify a good wife and able mother – exactly the kind of woman she longed to be. In her dreams, she would give birth to hundreds of children, and then stand in the middle of them, handing out apples. She would dress the children in pretty clothes and nourish them with the infinite streams of milk that flowed from her nipples. Her breasts could feed a multitude of children, and give men joy and pleasure. But today, these dreams were shattered. In other people's eyes, she was a fraud, a girl who tried to entice men with fake breasts. They thought they had seen through her games. Everyone had reached the same conclusion, even the young man in the office who read books every day preparing for his postgraduate exams.

'Let the mirror be the judge.' She kept her voice down, because behind the curtain her entire family were eating dinner. Her bed lay in a corner that was blocked off from the rest of the room by a curtain. She stayed awake all night. The next morning she swallowed some sleeping pills and took the day off work.

(As the blood donor discusses her story, the professional writer is suddenly reminded of the actress who jumped into the tiger's mouth. He asks, 'Do you think that the girl was trying to escape this world too?'

'No,' the blood donor replies. 'She was too young. She had nothing to escape from yet. She crumbled, not because of outside pressure, but because of her own weakness. If everyone were as feeble as her, we would have all lost our minds ages ago. She only ran through the streets naked once. It was no big deal.'

'Perhaps her story is just not worth writing,' the writer sighs wearily.

'You're wrong to think that every story must be connected with death. The problem is not death, but life, and life is just an act of endurance – you have to grit your teeth and get on with it. Just like I do. I put up with everything that life throws at me. I've suffered much more than you ever could in your carefree existence.'

The image of the girl's large breasts is still flashing through the writer's mind. The two raisin-coloured nipples stare at him entreatingly. Had the girl realised that it is already impossible in this world to distinguish the real from the fake, then perhaps she wouldn't have reached for the sleeping pills so frequently.)

When her family discovered that she was swallowing sleeping pills every night, and that her health was seriously deteriorating, they had no choice but to take her to hospital. The secretary and Chairwoman Fan took her flowers, her pay cheque, a bar of soap and a pair of silk gloves. She lay calmly in her hospital bed, staring blankly at the white walls. A few days after she returned home, she took all her clothes off and ran through the streets naked. Racked by shame, the family left town and set up home in a farm in the suburbs. But her past caught up with her, and her parents were forced to send her to live in their old village. Some years later she married a peasant, but when he learned about her reputation, he became violent, and frequently beat her to within a breath of her life.

Chairwoman Fan had still not retired by then. After the girl with big breasts resigned from work due to ill health, the secretary moved to her desk. The two cactus plants on the window sill grew so tall, they had to be moved outside into the corridor.

The Abandoner *or* The Abandoned

The conversations between the writer and the blood donor never lead anywhere. Instead of prolonging an argument, they often choose to leave it hanging in mid-air. It is interesting to note, however, that during tonight's conversation, the blood donor seems to be gaining the upper hand. The blood donor is by nature a profit seeker, believing that people should use all means possible to get what they need from this ugly world. The writer is an idealist, but when confronted by reality and his own failures, he overcomes his disappointment by adopting an air of indifference. He is a cripple who can think but not move. In his undernourished brain, he weaves the stories of the book he knows he will never write.

She emerged from between her mother's thighs just a month before the One Child Policy was launched.

(In his mind, the professional writer sees the father carrying his retarded child down the street with a furtive look in his eyes. The father's downturned mouth and sunken cheekbones speak of his despair. The little girl in his arms looks calm, but slightly perturbed. These two always seem to be on their way to somewhere.)

Since he was blood type A, and was born in the Year of the Ox, the father was both stubborn and shy. When he was twenty, a cabbage-faced old woman in a grain shop read the lines on his hand and told him he would never have a son. After he married, his wife produced a daughter with severe disabilities, and five years later, a second daughter, who was normal. The father then paid six yuan for a lame man called Zeng to read his fortune again. Zeng predicted that at forty-eight he would have a third daughter; at forty-nine, he would be promoted to a more senior position (he was now a middle-ranking accountant in the Municipal Treasury Board); at fifty, a gentleman would travel from the south-west and bring him good luck (he looked up all his friends and relatives who lived in the south-west, and discovered he had an uncle who was an ex-Guomindang general and was now living with a guerrilla force in Burma, although the family hadn't heard from him for over thirty years); at fifty-seven, his mother would pass away and his wife would die of lung disease; at sixty, he would meet a widow with blood type A who was born in the Year of the Sheep, and she would marry him and give him a fourth daughter. Death was destined to strike him in his sixty-third year. He once asked the lame man Zeng if there was any way he could prolong his life span by a few years – just two more years would do – but the fortune teller insisted that it was impossible to alter the course of fate.

The father was in fact more upset about the lack of a son to carry on his family name than about the shortness of his own life. He pushed the thought of the widow to the back of his mind, and focused all his attention on procuring a son. Since their first daughter had been born disabled, his wife's work unit had made an exception to the One Child Policy and granted her a quota of two children, but they would certainly never allow her to try for a third. The only way she could procure another pregnancy authorisation would be if one of their children happened to disappear. Had it not been for the family planning regulations, the couple would have been free to conceive one child after another until a son turned up, but as things stood, the accountant decided that his only hope lay in getting rid of his retarded daughter.

So he embarked on a battle against his fate. When his retarded daughter reached the age of seven, he grabbed her in his arms, carried her to a public park and attempted, unsuccessfully, to abandon her on a bench. After three further failed attempts, he took a day off work, hoping to finish the job properly. His future depended on ridding himself of her. Only with her gone could he try again for a son. The fortune tellers hadn't mentioned that his first daughter would be born retarded, or that the government was planning to introduce a One Child Policy. If he had known at the time how the future would unfold, he would have told his wife to get an abortion the moment she first found out she was pregnant.

His elder daughter looked similar to most children of the world who share her disability. She had a small flat head covered with thin downy hair, a broad and wrinkled forehead, tadpole-like eyes set deep into sallow sockets, a flat nose, and large nostrils that flared with each intake of breath. Her mouth was always open. Saliva and scraps of food would fall from it, drip down her small chin and collect in the creases of her thick neck. Her existence caused him only trouble.

During her seven years of life, she had acquired a few skills. For example, she knew to cry out when she felt the need to relieve herself, and had learned never to refuse any food or medicine. But she never lost her fear of being removed from the family's dank room and taken out into the fresh air. Whenever her father grabbed her in his arms and carried her to a place where an open expanse of sky could be seen, her hair stood on end, and her jaws clenched so hard it was impossible to wrench them apart. She had already spent a whole weekend alone in the woods, a night on a stone bench, six days in an orphanage in the countryside, and forty-eight hours on a train bound for the capital. Before each of these unhappy experiences, she would suddenly lose sight of her father and find herself alone. But in the end, she always managed to be rescued from danger and returned safely to the dark room that smelt of mud and rotten cabbage.

At the beginning of each journey, he had no idea whether he would succeed in abandoning her, but he was determined to continue his war against fate. For the sake of his future son, for the sake of the successful fertilisation of his wife's next egg cell, he would go ahead with his plan. He told himself that the only reason he looked after his daughter was to wait for an opportunity to get rid of her. For her, each journey they took together into the outside world was an opportunity to prove the resilience of her life force.

Although he had entered the Party in 1958, and had worked conscientiously for the following thirty years, he was still only a middle-ranking accountant. In the Cultural Revolution, he joined a political cell that failed to keep up with the changing times, and became outlawed by a rival cell. He ended up marrying an activist from the cell that had outlawed his. He made love to his wife in their dormitory room as the bullets pelted through the sky outside. Neither of them had much knowledge of sexual matters, other than the little they'd learned from various swear words, so the wife didn't become pregnant until their second year of marriage. The doctor told her that the child's defects were caused by excessive sexual activity during her pregnancy.

When he reached fifty, he resolved to focus more of his energies on the task of abandoning his elder daughter. He started taking his work less seriously. The fortune tellers had told him that considering the year in which he was born, he would only succeed in getting rid of his daughter if it was certain that someone would take her home and look after her. So he never abandoned his daughter if he thought there was any danger she might starve to death, or come to any harm. His failure in abandoning her was clearly linked to the year in which he was born. He was convinced that if he had been born in the Year of the Tiger or of the Chicken, he would be holding a baby son in his arms by now.

One morning, he left her alone in an open field outside town. He hid himself behind a bush in the distance, and observed her for an entire day. When the sun was setting in the west, he gave up hope of anyone coming to her rescue, so, faint with hunger, he ran over to her, grabbed her in his arms and carried her back home. He endured all kinds of hardships for her. One day he read an article about an orphanage in a neighbouring town. He took a day off work, travelled to the town and deposited his daughter at the reception desk of the orphanage, claiming he had found her on the street. The director of the orphanage told him the child was not necessarily an orphan, and that she would have to be handed over to the public security bureau. In a panic, the father explained that he had wanted to perform a good deed and emulate Lei Feng, but could do no more, as he had a train to catch. So the director agreed to take the child to the public security bureau herself. The next day, when he was gazing out of the window by his desk, the police of the neighbouring town telephoned him and asked him to collect his child from their bureau. So he took another day off work, much to his leader's consternation since it meant missing the department's weekly Party meeting. That afternoon, he waved goodbye to his wife and his younger daughter, who was now two years old, and set off on a journey to bring his elder daughter home.

('You live in your own small universe,' the blood donor tells the writer. 'You're stuck inside your mind, and this suitcase-like flat of yours. We're growing further and further apart.'

'What do you mean?'

'We have different values. I have surrendered to reality and made a success of my life. You put on a show of arrogance, but you are a failure, you live off this world's discarded dregs.')

Before abandoning his elder daughter, he always gave her a sleeping pill, afraid that if she were left awake, she might choke on her tears, or that her cries might attract a pack of wolves. Since she spent so much time out of doors, he even bought her a plastic coat to protect her from the rain. His wife was a typical Chinese woman. Each time he set off on a journey with his daughter in his arms, she always walked him to the door, her eyes filled with tears. Despite his repeated failures, she always managed to cry each time she waved him goodbye. She fully supported the course of action he had chosen to take. In the past, she herself had employed a go-between to arrange the sale of her elder daughter to an infertile couple, but unfortunately, when the couple discovered the child was retarded, they brought her back and demanded a refund.

The retarded child was subjected to an endless stream of trials and traumas, but always managed to escape with her life. Before she had taken her first step, she had survived two car accidents and a fall from a third-storey window. Later on, she found herself dropping from her bed onto the cement floor almost every night. Neighbours said that only a child who was blessed could survive so many accidents, and they predicted she would bring the family good fortune and prosperity. So for an entire year, the father gave up his attempts at abandoning her, and waited for his fortunes to turn.

But nothing happened, and the father became convinced once more that the future the lame man Zeng had predicted for him was cast in stone. The imminent end of his family line weighed heavily on his mind. He knew that if his wife exceeded her birth quota of two children, he would lose everything he had worked so hard to gain: his government job, his Party membership card, his room, his salary. The continued presence of his elder daughter in his family threatened every aspect of his existence.

In the end, he decided to take early retirement and concentrate all his waking hours on the mission to abandon his daughter. However, each time he tried to get rid of her, he felt his attachment to her grow deeper. In the past, he had hoped she would cooperate with him, and disappear quietly from his life so as to let him try again for a son. But as this hope diminished, she became his comforter and sympathiser. Although he caused her pain, she was the only person in this world who could forgive him.

As time went by, she became his closest friend. He couldn't help but pour out his heart to her, telling her about his marital problems, his concerns about world affairs, and the heartache he felt for all the pain he'd caused her. Knowing that she could say nothing in reply, he felt free to use the foulest language in her presence. As he grew aware of the futility of his efforts, he slowly lost control of his thoughts. Each time he attempted to abandon her, he felt as though he were in fact abandoning himself and the future that had been destined for him. But he was still determined to keep trying.

Sometimes he felt that it was his daughter who was dragging him through the town, rather than the other way round. Before each of his attempts at abandoning her, he seemed to hear her say: 'I consent to being abandoned. Over the years I have gained my own identity, and through your struggles with me you have learned some lessons about life. A father can fool a retarded child, but a retarded child can also fool her father. I have given a pattern to your life, a rhythm. You must understand that your mission will destroy you in the end. I have taught you things about yourself you would have preferred not to know. In a deranged world, only retarded people can find happiness. I share none of your commitments or responsibilities. I care nothing about the past or the future, or whether your sperm will ever meet another egg cell. I am not even sure whether I exist. If you were retarded, you would understand what I am saying. I wish you would give up this futile mission of yours. You've done your best for everyone. You have neither let me down, nor yourself down. There's nothing more you can do.'

As people became caught up in the changes brought about by the Open Door Policy, they began to talk less about this father and daughter who spent their lives being separated, then reunited. But everyone knew who they were. Occasionally they would see a man with freshly washed collar and cuffs (you could tell at a glance he was a cadre) emerge from behind the municipal museum, holding a retarded child in his arms. He would cross the pedestrian flyover, then proceed through the new urban district, heading not for the seaside park, but for the open fields beyond. When he reached his destination, he would place the child down by the side of the road, then squat behind a tree ten or so metres away. Passers-by noticed that when he was squatting there, the lines on his face seemed to disappear. But as soon as someone walked over and laid their hands on his 'lost property', he would jump to his feet, charge over and scoop her up in his arms. In this town, he became the retarded child's only protector.

What will happen to me tomorrow? the professional writer wonders. Perhaps I'll bump into those two on the street, and see the look of despair in the father's eyes. The writer's mind turns to the quiet waitress with long hair who works in the noodle shop where he goes to eat rice congee. He likes to gaze at her. She is brimming with life, but has a reserved and peaceful demeanour. He wonders how he can manage to work her into his novel too.

The Carefree Hound *or* The Witness

His bark often woke me from my sleep. It sounded different from the bark he used during our conversations: it was the bark of a dog. In the two months following his death, his bark continued to wake me. I'll never recover from the fact that I was not with him when he died.

(The professional writer strokes his cigarette lighter and remembers the day he had lunch with the painter in the cafeteria of the municipal museum. The painter stared at him and asked, 'Do you think my dog will be reincarnated again? How come he could talk like you and me? I've never told anyone the truth about him before, not even my girlfriend. I'll tell you now, but you may not believe it.')

I never saw what he looked like when he was dead. When I returned from my conference trip, he was already being transformed into a museum exhibit. Secretary Wang, the director of the museum, never told me the story behind his death, he just sent an officer up to my room to criticise me for secretly rearing a dog. The children downstairs told me they'd seen the dog being beaten to death by the old carpenter who lives on the fourth floor. They even led me to the alleged scene of the crime. They pointed to a dirty patch on the concrete floor and claimed it was the dog's blood. I examined the patch carefully, and discovered that it was in fact a paint stain left behind by the decorators a few years ago. So I didn't tackle the old carpenter about the subject. One day, Secretary Wang saw a picture I'd taken of the dog and said, 'Well, if you didn't want this to happen, you shouldn't have let your dog piss in the lift.' I came straight out with it, and asked him whether the old carpenter had been responsible for my dog's death. Secretary Wang glanced at the door and said, 'Did that security officer pay you a visit in the end? He was furious to hear that you were keeping a dog.'

When I asked him again how the dog had died, Secretary Wang seemed to change into a moth. His eyes became smaller and smaller, then he turned his back on me and flitted away through the open door. I could tell that his arse was no cleaner than any of the others I see in the public latrines. When I returned from my conference trip, the kennel was empty and there was no smell of urine on the terrace. The piece of cloth I had cut from the blanket on my bed was still lying in his basket, but it was infested with ants now. When I peered down, the ants looked up at me, then continued to race though the forest of woollen threads, as fast as the people in the streets below.

I crawled out of the kennel and started searching the roof terrace for any signs of the dog's presence. The terrace is huge. There are so many chimneys sticking up from it, it looks like a forest of dead trees, or a field of gravestones. Some of the chimneys are over fifty years old and built in the shape of a cross. My room is in the tall clock tower on the edge of the terrace. It has a small window that looks out onto the streets below. Before my girlfriend committed suicide, she often came to visit me. She complained that the terrace was like a graveyard, and the clock tower like the house of the cemetery guard. She hated all the pipes that cut across the roof, she was always tripping over them. But my dog leaped happily across the terrace for more than two years without complaining once, and he only had three legs.

The clock doesn't strike the hour any longer. During the Cultural Revolution, a Maoist cell called 'Army of Millions' took control of the tower and removed some parts of the clock to make weapons for use in their battles against the rival Maoist cell, 'The Expulsion of Enemy Factions Brigade'. In the past, policemen all over town used to time their shifts by the clock. You can see its face from any road in the city. Likewise, I can see the entire town from my terrace, including the new urban district by the sea. When I get up in the morning and step out onto the terrace, I can see my former classmates and other people I know squeezing onto buses or eating breakfast at street stalls. Some who've made it into the office already and are trapped in a political meeting, wink up at me through their windows. When they finish work, I shout out to them, and they all shout back to me. It's easier than using a telephone.

My dog was born up there.

(This was obviously impossible, the writer thinks to himself. For a start, no female dog had ever set foot on the terrace. The truth is, his dog was in fact born in the suburbs, in a yard outside a private crematorium. Only there was it possible for dogs to produce puppies that were so similar to men. The yard was haunted by the spirits of the dead. The dogs took pity on some of them, and allowed them to reincarnate themselves in their offspring.)

When I saw he only had three legs, I was overwhelmed with pity and decided to take him into my care. He wasn't steady on his feet. If he was standing up, I would sometimes prod his front leg and he'd topple to the ground. After a few months, he learned that if he splayed his legs out in a tripod position, he was less likely to fall. The next time I tried to topple him, he curled his lip and said, 'Don't waste your energy, my friend.' I was so startled to hear the dog speak, I felt like running away. But before I'd had a chance to move, he sighed, 'I'm just telling you – give it a rest.'

'Are you really a dog?' I asked.

'Well, what are you?'

'A man, of course.'

'Well I'm a dog then. But I must have been a man in a previous life, otherwise how would I be able to speak your language?'

'Which man do you think you were?'

'Go and check the municipal death register, if you're so

interested. Why should I tell you? One thing I will say is that I've lived in this town for over a hundred years. I would never have guessed I'd come back this time as a three-legged dog, though. What a joke!'

'Who were you in your past life?' I repeated, my body still shaking like a leaf.

'I'm not sure. There's no way of knowing. All I do know is that I didn't want to return as a human in my next life. I don't mind being a dog, it's just a shame I have one leg missing.'

We got on well together. As soon as I finished my work in the museum, I would run upstairs to the terrace and see him waiting for me outside his kennel. I'd jump over the maze of pipes, unlock my door and let him in. I would paint for a few hours, then we'd retire to bed to read books and discuss various matters of the day. He read nearly every book in my room, apart from the ones on the highest shelf. I forbade him to touch those because I was afraid that their contents might corrupt his mind, and besides, I couldn't bear the thought of him overtaking me. I also insisted he made sure the door to our terrace was locked before he raised his voice or barked. Three of the museum's staff, including the old carpenter and his son the plumber, belonged to the dog extermination brigade. If news had reached them that there was a dog on my terrace, they would have had the authority to search my tower then eat any dog they found. They always ate the dogs they killed – their leaders only required them to hand in the dog's head.

I work as an illustrator for the municipal museum's natural history section. My task is to make sketches of all the stuffed animals that are exhibited in the museum. The job is much better than any my old classmates were assigned, so I consider myself very fortunate. After the survivor moved in with me (that's the name the dog gave himself), I was afraid he might jeopardise my career. So to protect myself, I began to work more assiduously, and stepped up my efforts to join the Party. But the dog died in the end, and all that survives of him now is his beautiful hide.

(The writer remembers the blank expression on the painter's face when he recounted his story in the cafeteria. It was impossible to know whether he was telling the truth or not. Perhaps the survivor was just an extension of himself. When the writer asked him if he really believed the dog had lived on that terrace, the painter grunted impatiently and said, 'His kennel is still up there. You saw it yourself.')

When I returned from the conference, I found the dog had been taken from my terrace and placed in the museum workshop. I heard that he would be travelling to Beijing the following month to take part in a national exhibition. When I first paid him a visit in the carpenter's workshop, his coat seemed softer and shinier than it was when he was alive. His sad-looking eyes had been replaced by a pair of shiny glass balls. His ears used to droop, but now that they had dried, they stood up perkily on end. The carpenter had stuffed so much cotton wool into his stomach, he looked like a pregnant bitch. Around him lay piles of dead animals waiting to be stuffed. A leopard with glass eyes leaned against the wall, its four limbs still nailed to a wooden frame; a gutted fox waiting to be put outside to dry in the sun stared sadly out of the open window. Compared to the dismembered and lacerated pheasants, bald eagles and pythons by his side, the survivor looked very animated. But however hard I tried, I could never associate the dead survivor with the dog I had known.

My roof terrace is huge. When you stand by the edge, you can see the whole town spread out below. The survivor could spy on every home in every street. In over two years, he never once left the roof: that's to say, he lived his entire life in mid-air. He kept his distance from the rest of humanity and refused to enter their world. While three thousand dogs perished at the hands of the town's extermination brigade, he was able to survive two years up there, thanks to me and the distance he kept from the crowds. He often saw his fellow dogs being chased and battered by the authorities, and it upset him. But I must admit that on seven occasions I was tempted to hand him over to the police, as I knew this might improve my chances of being awarded Party membership. By looking after him, I sometimes felt I was bringing disgrace upon the Party. He often spouted reactionary ideas that would later trouble my mind during the political study classes at work.

He matured a great deal during his two years with me, and learned a few elegant turns of phrase. He developed a deep insight into all things that had happened and had not yet happened. His shiny black coat and droopy ears gave him the look of a foreign lawyer. His unusual bald head and long grey whiskers added to this air of a wise elder. He secretly saw himself as a holy messenger and prophet. He was optimistic about China's implementation of the Open Door Policy, and agreed with the authorities that exhibitions of nude paintings weren't in tune with the social climate of our country. When the Central Committee announced that they'd given a Chinese woman their personal consent to marry a French citizen, he praised their courage. He argued that the Responsibility System could save socialism, and applauded the government's moves to encourage foreign companies to invest in our country. I asked him whether this policy would be tantamount to allowing foreign capitalists to take over the Chinese economy, but he just laughed at me coldly. I admit I grew very fond of him. Every day I brought back delicious things for him to eat and drink. I lost hours of sleep, worrying that one day the police would find him and take him away. My attachment to him was so deep that I managed to sit through my girlfriend's suicide performance without shedding a tear.

Our conversations were fascinating. He told me stories from the Greek legends and fables from the Bible. His topics ranged from the ancient world to the modern, from China to the West. His imagination was boundless. It was a pleasure to spend my evenings with him. A few days before we witnessed the gang rape that took place on the streets below us, I asked him what changes dogs would make if they were placed in control of this town. He said: 'First and foremost, we would eliminate the dog extermination brigade. Dogs are not to blame for rabies – we are just the innocent carriers of the virus. The dogs of this town would be granted the same privileges that dogs in foreign countries enjoy: they would be issued with dog collars made of real leather, and warm woollen dog coats. We would encourage humans to follow our example and restrict themselves to mating seasons, so as to improve the quality of their species. We would protect your borders, allow you freedom to travel, and freedom to set up opposition parties.'

His drooping ears flapped contentedly, and he continued: 'Our dog government will send your politicians and generals to the countryside to produce high quality meat for us. Their salaries and status will be second only to ours. If I were the mayor of this town, I'd ban all political meetings and study sessions, and I'd urge people to walk on all fours, as modestly and unassumingly as us. I would also scrap the practice of blasting exercise music through the town every morning, so that people could have a lie-in if they wanted to.'

'And what will our duties be in the new society?'

'To serve the dogs,' he said. 'You will simply have to change your motto from "Serve the People" to "Serve the Dogs". Your main responsibility will be to provide us with food and drink. As long as you don't start wasting your time with useless political meetings, we will cause you no harm. Remember – a dog is a man's best friend, and a man is a dog's best partner.'

A few days later, as we looked down on the girl being raped in the streets below, the dog went back to this conversation and said, 'But there's one thing we'll insist on when we come to power: we will ban all cars, trucks and bicycles from the town, to ensure that dogs are free to cross the roads when they wish.'

That day, the traffic in the streets below was blocked solid. At the intersection, a group of young men had pinned a girl to the ground and were raping her again and again. They had ripped all the clothes from her body and flung them in the air.

('Gang rapes are becoming a common sight in the cities and towns of China,' the blood donor tells his friend. 'In Shanghai last year, there was a gang rape that lasted two hours. The traffic in Nanjing Road came to a standstill. The crowd of spectators was so thick, the police were unable to reach the scene of the crime. When the girl managed to break free at last, she clambered up to the traffic warden's watchtower and begged for help, but the warden refused to open his door for her. The boys then pulled her down and began to rape her all over again. I read that the girl later suffered a nervous breakdown. After the rapists were finally arrested, the ringleader was driven to a sports stadium and executed by a firing squad.')

The girl below us finally managed to break free. She climbed up to the traffic warden's watchtower to beg for help, but the warden refused to open his door. He said he was only responsible for the traffic. Before she had time to argue, one of her attackers pulled her down again and pressed her to the ground. From the terrace, he looked like a mechanical toy as he thrust himself in and out of her body. His partners stood around him in a circle, pushing the onlookers back.

'They've brought the traffic to a stop,' the survivor said. 'When dogs mate, our friends don't stand about gaping at us like that.'

'This shouldn't be happening!' I shouted. 'It's a disgrace!'

A large crowd had gathered on the streets. People stared out from the windows of the surrounding apartment blocks. A mob stormed onto the pedestrian flyover above the intersection even though it hadn't yet been officially opened to the public. In the scrum, a few people were squeezed over the edge and fell onto the crowd below. Time and again, the girl's white bra could be seen flying into the air, then floating gently to the ground. Her red knickers were flung so high, they became caught on one of the lamps on the flyover. Two young men challenged each other to bring them down. As they climbed the flyover's cement legs, the crowd burst into applause. The thinner of the two made it to the top first. He grabbed hold of the knickers, kissed them, then hurled them back down into the crowd. A man below caught them and tossed them into the air again. For a minute or so, they hovered above the crowd like a dove, before falling once more to the ground.

'Humans have powerful herding instincts. It's no wonder you need to be controlled. You'd be much better off living together like ants, antelopes and moths, rather than shutting yourselves up in separate rooms.'

'I don't understand those people,' I said. 'They must have lost their minds.'

'Perhaps other animals are equally indifferent to the suffering of their own kind, but I doubt any of them could find as many ways to inflict pain as men have. It seems to me that man is the lowest beast of the lot.'

By that time, the dog had already lived on the terrace for nearly two years.

'Look at the secret glee on the faces of the crowd,' he said. 'Everyone can see what's happening, but no one is prepared to put a stop to it. Now you know the evil that lies hidden behind the blank faces you pass every day on the streets. Wherever a street lamp goes out at night, a woman is sure to be raped. Look at all those men down there. It usually takes a lot to make them blush, but they're so excited now, their faces are bright red. I can smell the blood rushing to their genitals.'

'This is nothing!' I cried. 'When Chairman Mao came out to greet the Red Guards in Tiananmen Square, the crowds were far more excited than this.'

'What was so exciting about seeing your Chairman?'

'Just imagine it. We grew up seeing his image plastered over every wall, book, newspaper and film. He was the only thing people ever talked about. So it was only natural that when we were able to see him at last with our own eyes, the emotion would send us into a frenzy.'

'But when it comes down to it, Chairman Mao was just a human being like any other,' the dog said.

'If it weren't for me, there would be no you. If it weren't for Chairman Mao, there would be no today,' I countered. His reactionary ideas were beginning to anger me.

'And what's so good about today?' He puckered his lips and

pointed them to the scene unfolding below. The girl had been pushed down again, and was being groped by a sea of hands. Her voice had died, and the tears that drenched her hair had run dry. A gang of youths climbed onto the roof of a stationary bus to get a better view. The men nearest the naked girl pressed her legs down, and kicked each other back as they fought to climb on top of her.

'I'm sure those thugs come from bad family backgrounds,' I said.

'What point does human existence serve?' the dog asked pompously.

'That sounds like a phrase from one of the books on my top shelf!' I snapped. 'I hope you haven't been reading those books behind my back!'

A blush rose to the dog's cheeks, and he turned his face away in shame. He had been lying in the sunniest corner of the terrace all morning, his head resting on a metal pipe, his front leg (which grew from the middle of his chest) stretched lazily forward. When the warm breeze stroked across his shiny coat, a loose hair would detach itself and drift down towards the mob below. By midday the crowd was still growing. A coach became marooned behind the stationary bus, and was unable either to retreat or advance. The girl was now too weak to put up a struggle. When the men who were sprawled on top of her heard the siren of a police car, they jumped up and tried to hide themselves in the crowd, but no space opened for them. The girl wrapped her arms over her thighs and chest as though she were trying to keep herself warm. When her attackers finally managed to make their escape, the crowd closed in on her. Hundreds of hands squeezed and fondled her body. She lay on the road as limp as a dying rabbit, and shuddered convulsively.

'That young man who just ran off is the girl's boyfriend,' the survivor said.

'How do you know that?' I shouted. The revolutionary anthem 'Chairman Mao's Brilliance Lights Up the World' was now blaring from the loudspeakers on the flyover.

'Last month I saw them strolling together down Liberation

Street. They continued to Fifth Street, then cut through East Peace Street to West Peace Street. In the early hours of the morning, I spotted them emerging from Friendship Park.'

'If he's her boyfriend, how could he bring three men along with him to rape her?'

'Men possess a trait that no dogs have.'

'What's that?'

'Jealousy,' he said, scratching his whiskers. The horde of spectators was becoming restless. People were continually pushing in from the surrounding streets and alleys. The policemen climbed out of their car and charged into the crowd. The people they squeezed out of the way soon found new gaps to fill. A melodious tenor's voice rang through the loudspeakers, singing:

Our beloved Party, you have been like a mother to me. You've taught me to love our country and encouraged me to study hard. A joyful tomorrow waves its hand to me, beckoning me onwards . . .

The noise of the orchestra and the police siren reverberated through the air above the crowd.

'Are you suggesting she was unfaithful to him, then?'

'Human beings shouldn't be allowed to fall in love,' he said with great feeling.

'What's happening below is just a chance occurrence,' I said, trying to defend the human race.

'Look how you treated your girlfriend!'

'She was an exceptional case.'

The survivor smiled. When he smiled, his eyes twinkled and his whiskers quivered up and down.

Another batch of policemen in white uniforms charged through the streets. It was decided that the builders' cabin on the pedestrian flyover should be converted into the temporary headquarters of the crowd dispersal unit. Four officers hauled a bench into the cabin, and a waitress from a nearby restaurant delivered a tray with tea cups and a thermos of hot water. This was a sign that the town leaders were about to arrive, and sure enough, a few minutes later, two limousines with red flags on the bonnet arrived from the municipal Party committee building, and three black cars with tinted windows turned up from the public security bureau. The vehicles cut a wide path through the crowd and came to a halt below the flyover. The officials stepped out, shook hands and pointed jovially at each other's bulging stomachs. Then they climbed up to the flyover, and with a great show of ceremony, entered the cabin to discuss how to resolve the situation.

The dog licked his outstretched leg and curled his tongue around the swollen red patch above his claws. The patch was bare. It looked like a wound, although neither of us could explain how he had got it. Leaning his head back again on the metal pipe he said sleepily, 'It will be another two hours before the police finally get to the girl. She will be as good as dead by then.'

'But look, they have nearly reached her.'

'No, they're not moving. They're just standing still now, waiting for the leaders in the cabin to come to a decision.'

I took a closer look and saw that the officers were indeed standing still. The crowd appeared to have calmed down a little, although everyone seemed uncomfortable at having to stand so close together. Some men took out cigarettes from their pockets and offered them to the policemen. Then they passed their lighters around and started discussing Tian Gu's new hairstyle in her latest film, *The Happy Revolution*.

'If those hooligans were dogs, how would you deal with them?' I asked the survivor.

'The fact is dogs would never commit such a crime.'

'Still, the committee leaders are doing a fine job. They've charged into the thick of things and resolved to sort this matter out in person.'

'Of course, the editorial of tomorrow's newspaper will claim that the secretary of the municipal Party committee left his sick-bed to rush here and put an end to this hooligan riot. You are lowly creatures, far inferior to us dogs. You try to adopt our civilised behaviour and our sense of morality and justice, but in your hearts all you think about is money and food coupons.'

The dog seemed to ignore for a moment the noise booming from the streets below. He turned his head away. 'Can you do me a favour?' he said, lowering his gaze to the ground. 'I saw some spare ribs in a dustbin on Serve the People Road. There was still some meat left on the bones.'

I kept silent.

'They were obviously stewed in some thick, spicy sauce,' he said, still averting his eyes. He took a gulp of water from his bowl, then pointed his nose into the air and sniffed the breeze.

'You still haven't finished that joint I brought back from the cafeteria yesterday.'

'It was revolting,' he moaned. 'You know I don't like mutton bones.'

'But I can only get bones from the Muslim section now.'

He bowed his head again and sighed.

In the streets below, the crowd started scattering like a swarm of ants. More policemen and security officers arrived at the scene. Then a regiment of PLA soldiers, fronted by two army tanks, suddenly appeared from nowhere, and began to drive back the remaining hordes chanting 'Socialism is good!' in thick Henan accents.

'They've caught one of the rapists,' I cried.

'Did you see those people demonstrating in the streets last week?' The dog seemed distracted. He was probably still thinking about the spare ribs in the dustbin.

A huge grey cloud moved through the sky, and the streets darkened. The girl was wrapped in a blanket and escorted into a police van. On the flyover above the intersection, the leaders' meeting was approaching a conclusion.

'She shouldn't have worn that tight skirt,' I muttered. 'None of the women in our museum are allowed to wear tight skirts.'

The dog gazed up at the clouds and said, 'In two minutes the rain will fall. It was the low air pressure this morning that made those boys lose their minds.'

Raindrops cut through the sunlit sky like threads of nylon. The dog shook the water from his coat and stood up. 'The rain is clean, but when it reaches the earth it turns into mud,' he said.

'Why not just enjoy the sight of the rain and forget about the mud?'

'I live in the clouds, so of course I can just look at the rain. But your feet are stuck on the ground, so you can't ignore the mud.'

'You dogs are so lucky. You can roam the world without a care, while we must spend our days earning money to pay our rent, buy jumpers, raincoats and thermal underwear. If we want to keep our jobs, we must control our behaviour and deny ourselves the flights of fancy and reactionary meditations you indulge in. We have to study the newspapers every day to ensure we take the correct political line. Our skins are so thin, we have to wear clothes, and when these clothes are ripped from us, we become like naked pigs, or that girl on the street below. We depend on our elegant wrappings. We have to conceal our true natures if we want to survive.'

'You sound as though you've caught a cold,' the dog whined, paying no attention to what I had said.

When I returned from the conference and discovered the survivor had died, my spirits crumbled. Every day I stared at my paintbrush, but was unable to lift it to my canvas. I longed to contract a fatal disease, or to perish in some natural disaster. If I'd been a drinker, I would have drunk myself to oblivion. How nice that would have been. To stop myself from dreaming about him at night, I turned my bed round so that my head pointed south. I'd read in a magazine that this keeps nightmares at bay, and also improves your complexion and delays the onset of grey hairs. Although I did indeed suffer fewer nightmares after that, my dreams became more erotic. One night, I dreamed I was flying through the air, chasing after a fat girl's bottom. After I grabbed hold of it, I discovered it belonged to the woman who plucks dead ducks in the museum's cafeteria.

Since he passed away, I haven't cried once, or encountered one setback that might have allowed me to release a strong emotion. The world has carried on as usual. Although my parents are over eighty, they are in fine health. My classmates are still living dull, uneventful lives. My girlfriend's suicide has almost vanished from my mind. Apart from me, everyone seems at peace with themselves.

In memory of his perceptive gaze, I bought myself a telescope. Now I can see the world of men as he saw it. Sometimes I even pass comments on events taking place below.

The town is quiet and orderly now. Bright red boxes have been attached to every street corner to collect citizens' reports of uncivilised behaviour. The municipal Party committee has banned pedestrians from shouting, laughing or running in the streets, and insists that they only walk outside in groups of less than four. If a group exceeds four members, it has to split in two. The committee has also arranged for cultural troupes to visit local work units to educate employees on the virtues of polite behaviour and assess their understanding of modern citizenship. Our work unit failed to make the grade because two old comrades from the finance department walked down the street taking strides that were judged to be either too large or too small.

When I look down from the terrace, the pedestrians seem to squirm through the streets as slowly as maggots. The only time I ever see a crowd is in the morning, when the pensioners are doing their exercises in Red Scarf Park.

I often sit on the terrace gazing at the clouds in the blue sky. They seem to have been hanging in the same position for months. I'm painting again now, but my inspiration has gone. I've messed around with the canvas on my easel for so long that from a distance it looks like a dirty apron.

The other day, I borrowed a guitar from an old classmate, and played a mournful tune on the spot beside the kennel where I used to sit and chat with the dog. I thrummed the strings and the tinkling melody drifted into the air. I thrummed again, but this time the strings produced no sound. In the evening, the head of the museum's security department came up and told me not to play my guitar on the terrace again. He said the State Security Department had confiscated the noise from my instrument, and from now on I'd have to content myself with listening to the radio. He took the guitar from me, but to my great relief, didn't ask me to write a self-criticism letter.

If only the survivor could see how clean the streets are now. He wouldn't recognise the place. I often think back on those warm summer evenings when we lay on the terrace, the sea breeze stroking my skin and his fur. He would give me his canine view of the world, and criticise humans for not being more like dogs. This angered me. Since dogs don't drive cars or wear clothes, he argued that cars were unnecessary and launderettes a waste of time. 'And your cinemas are so noisy,' he said one night, 'they give me a headache.'

'Thank goodness God never let dogs rule the world,' I replied.

'Man's habit of standing upright is disgusting. Your leaders address the crowds with their chests and genitals on full display. When we want to speak, we just lift our heads up. It's much more polite that way.' He then outlined the policies a future dog government would introduce to reform human behaviour.

'It's true our leaders address the people standing upright,' I consented, 'but at least they are polite enough to wear clothes. You may bend over when you speak, but everyone can still see the genitals dangling between your legs. If ever the day came when you dogs were to gain power, I'd prefer to climb onto my roof and turn into a mouse rather than submit myself to your rule.'

'At least the dogs would do a better job of ruling this country than your government has done.' When the stars came out at night, his eyes were piercingly bright.

'We have transcended the animal world through our invention of speech. Look at our wonderful libraries!' I said, pointing at the floodlit public library below.

'We dogs learn through a slow accumulation of experience. We are more sensitive and astute than you. For example, I know what tomorrow's weather will be, when the next earthquake will strike, which mushrooms are poisonous, and which person is going where. We glide effortlessly through this world, learning as we go. But it takes you twenty years before you know enough to allow you to leave home. Most dogs are already dead by then. A three-month-old puppy knows more than any of your university professors. Dogs don't need colleges or libraries – we're happy to leave those places to you to while away your time in.'

'Will dogs be allowed to get married when you take control?' I asked.

'The sex life of dogs is seasonal: we only have intercourse during the spring. And when we rise to power, we will preserve this custom. Your excessive sex drive is the root cause of today's social instability. Look at that building opposite us! At this moment, from the ground floor to the eighth, nearly every couple is having intercourse. Those two on the third floor have done it twice tonight. They did the same last night, and the night before, with just a few changes of position, that's all.'

The building opposite was an apartment block for the staff of the Municipal Cultural Department. As the lights were turned off in each room, the dog would smell the sour scent of body fluids wafting from the open windows.

'I'm quite fond of that man who lives on the eighth floor, though,' the dog confessed. 'When he opens his window, I can smell the jar of ink next to the musty books on his desk. He hasn't slept with a woman for months, but on Sunday nights, delicious smells of meat and fish always flow from his room.'

'He's a friend of mine – a professional writer. On his salary, he could never afford to support a wife.'

'Well you manage to support me on your meagre pay,' he said guiltily. 'There's a woman down there who is in love with him, although she still goes out with other men. I can see her thought waves racing towards his room right now.'

I looked to where he was pointing. 'Do you mean that old-fashioned building over there?' I asked.

'She has spent the last few nights drinking with a chain-smoker. When tobacco smoke and alcohol fumes mix together, it smells like old mutton.'

At night the town looks cold and desolate. The survivor discovered that when people are lying down in the dark, they become more active than they are when the lights are on. The noises of copulation and the sour smells of body fluids often made his stomach turn.

'I can't bear it when there's no breeze at night,' he said.

'Men could never agree to relinquishing the joys of marriage.'

'All you want to do is eat, have sex and go shopping. These activities all require the participation of others – not just one person, but a crowd of them. You need to huddle in towns and cities to escape the emptiness in your hearts.'

'I work myself to the bone for you, to care for all your needs.'

'All you do is bring me a little water every morning. And you always end up drinking some of it yourself.'

'Think how many times I've had to clear up your messes! When you pissed in the doorway last week, you plonked my wash bowl over the puddle to try and hide it from me, but I still cleaned it up for you.'

'You smashed my chamber pot that day – I had no choice but to piss on the ground.'

'Sweep those scraps of bones back onto your plate, will you,' I grunted.

'Can you pass me my bowl of water, please?'

He put his mouth to the bowl and took a large gulp. Then he looked up and said, 'It's hot today. If only you knew how uncomfortable I get in this thick coat of fur.'

'There's a fan in my office. It makes a nice breeze.'

'I'd love a chance to sit in front of it.' When he drifted into his fantasies, his tail would start wagging of its own accord.

'You know I could never let you leave this terrace.'

He licked the water from his lips, then edged forward and started licking my feet.

'It wouldn't be safe to take you down,' I said, pulling my foot away from him. 'The streets are full of policemen, even at night.'

He cocked his head flirtatiously and whined, 'Go and find me a little companion then.'

I roared with laughter. 'You want a bitch, don't you? You rascal!'

Hearing this, he pounced up excitedly onto my lap, almost knocking me to the ground.

('Unfortunately, I never managed to satisfy this desire of his,' the painter admitted to the writer. 'In his entire life, he never so much as talked with a member of his own species, let alone did anything else with them.' The writer looked up at him and said, 'You must miss him very much.')

When I think back to the days we spent together, my mood lifts a little. Last Saturday I attended the weekly political meeting at work, and as usual I spent the time having conversations with the dog in my mind. The chairman was using a brand-new microphone, but his speech was as monotonous as ever.

'. . . Our Party has a glorious future. Yes. Comrade Deng Xiaoping's latest report stressed this unequivocally. Our Party is undergoing change, enormous change. The Party centre has stated that the three sectors of society hold equal importance, and this is the view both of the wider Party, and of the people. Yes. Our determination must not falter. Five years may seem long, but I can assure you, they will pass very quickly. The war against Japan lasted only eight years . . .' Half the audience in the hall was staring at the chairman standing on the podium, the other half had closed their eyes and escaped into their own thoughts. Three women at the back had got their knitting out and were having a quiet chat. 'Our nation at present is united. Comrades, we must endeavour to –' The microphone suddenly let out a deafening squeak. The chairman was so startled he dropped his tea cup on the floor and it shattered into pieces. All the eyes in the hall focused on the broken fragments. There was still an hour and a half to go. 'Time is short, comrades, so I'll press on and skip to the fifth point. Our Party overcame many difficulties during the three years of economic slowdown. This proves that there is no crisis our Party cannot surmount. Think about it comrades – were it not for the leadership of the Party, our nation would be moving backwards, yes, backwards. Our Party is the best party in the world. It's deeply embedded in the hearts and minds of the people . . .'

No matter how hard I tried, I couldn't concentrate on his words. I'm afraid that my political resolve has been weakening. In the past, I used to pore over each document my leaders sent down to me. I complied with every decision they made concerning my personal relationships and political studies. I was one of the lucky ones. Because my parents joined the Party before Liberation, and had lived in a Soviet controlled area, I was absolved from attending the re-education camps that my classmates were sent to. At school, I was as skinny as a dried pickle and the shortest boy in the year, but because of my family background I was appointed chairman of the student union in the first week of term. I took the position very seriously, and participated in every school activity. In the morning, I ran two circuits of the playing field to give my complexion a healthy glow, and at night I practised my political speeches. After I left school, I became even more conscientious. When Premier Zhou Enlai announced that smoking was patriotic, I smoked ten cigarettes in one day, although in the afternoon I felt so ill I had to be carried to the sickbay. That show of patriotism was almost sufficient to secure my Party membership. But unfortunately, I never succeeded in acquiring an addiction to tobacco.

After the rape incident, the dog often asked me when the pedestrian flyover would be officially opened. Sometimes I would read out articles for him from the local paper. One night, as the traffic wardens' voices were booming above the roar of the streets below, I read out an article entitled 'Good Prospects for the Flyover'. It said: 'Having received 170 complaints from the public concerning the construction of the flyover, the provincial authorities sent a team to the site yesterday to investigate the problem. The thirteen members of the team promised to assess the situation objectively and reject any bribes or special treatment. They were true to their word. After they arrived at the train station, they declined the use of the limousines sent by the municipal Party committee and chose instead to travel to the site by public bus. The crowds they met along the way approved of their frugal and upright attitude. When they reached the site, the team enquired about the number of traffic incidents that have occurred under the flyover this month. They visited the newly established rescue centre and arranged for a doctor who neglected to deal with the dislocated shoulder of a crash victim to be sent away for interrogation. In their final report, the team pointed out that the political study meetings held in the rescue centre on Monday, Wednesday and Friday afternoons create severe disruptions to medical care, and they suggested that this matter should be looked into . . .'

'It seems that the investigation team has solved many problems,' I said, looking up from the page.

'If they hadn't built that flyover in the first place, there would never have been so many accidents,' the dog complained.

'At least the municipal authorities are working hard to put matters right.'

'Surely they realise that the only way to solve this problem now is to hurry up and open the flyover to the public.'

Did he really imagine that the municipal Party committee had the power to decide when the flyover was to be opened? He was so naïve. Only the Central Committee can make such decisions. And they're responsible for running the entire country – they have far more pressing issues to think about than solving our pedestrian flyover problem.

'Don't you understand the difference between the higher echelons and the people?' I said. 'Would dogs ever dare question their superiors? Your arrogance is monstrous. Our leaders built the flyover to relieve congestion. How dare you turn things around and claim they are to blame for today's traffic problems?'

'You lead a miserable life. It's not much better than a dog's.'

'Don't you know that the more miserable you are, the longer you live?' I said, exasperated by his ignorance.

The survivor always enjoyed feasting his eyes on the accidents that took place on the streets below. He once predicted that over three hundred people a year would die in traffic incidents caused by the construction of the pedestrian flyover. Never in my life will I forgive him this mistake. Admittedly, in the early days, the construction of the flyover did indeed lead to a dramatic increase in road casualties. Pedestrians would flock to it, hoping to make a safe crossing, but on finding it wasn't yet open to the public, they would end up charging across the intersection at its busiest point. The survivor told me he could see the ghosts of the dead flitting between the flyover's concrete legs.

But after the rape incident, the town leaders took steps to ease the problem. They erected metal huts on the flyover to house a medical rescue centre. Anyone injured in an accident below is promptly carried to the rescue hut and given free emergency care. The scheme has been a great success. The municipal Party committee has praised the nurses' contribution to revolutionary humanitarianism, and awarded them prizes and certificates of merit. Although citizens are still denied the pleasure of using the flyover to cross the street, and people continue to be crushed to death by the busy traffic, the flyover still has its merits. When my classmate broke his leg at work, he managed to get it bandaged free of charge in the flyover's rescue centre. I often visit the survivor in the museum to tell him of the great progress that has been made, but I have to make sure my colleagues aren't watching – they are always making jokes about me. One time they saw me tuck into a meat pie at lunch, and they said, 'Be careful, that's dog meat.' I felt queasy for days after that.

When he was alive, the survivor prophesied that the flyover wouldn't open to the public until 1992, but there's still a year and a half to go, and there are already signs that the official opening will take place soon: the flyover curfew officers have been replaced by a flyover management team, and the local traffic wardens have been issued with brand-new uniforms.

The flyover was originally scheduled to be opened last year, on the first anniversary of the dog's death. The Central Committee wanted to make the flyover a symbol of the Open Door Policy. They decided its opening should be tied in with Ceauşescu's visit to China, and that it should be named the

Sino-Romanian Friendship Flyover. They instructed the town leaders to take great pains to ensure the opening was a success. The authorities decked the railings with little red flags, in preparation for the arrival of Ceauşescu, who had been invited to open the flyover during a visit organised to celebrate the twinning of this town with an industrial city in his country. The government sent engineers to the site to search for any hidden bombs, and plain-clothed security officers patrolled the surrounding streets to check that no one was pasting counter-revolutionary flyers to the walls. But unfortunately, Ceauşescu was assassinated a few days before he was due to leave, so the ceremony had to be called off.

When the Campaign to Learn from Lei Feng was launched, a broadcasting cabin was built on the flyover next to the metal huts, and every citizen in town who couldn't afford to buy a radio jumped with joy. People were able to stand in the streets and listen to the broadcasts for free. They could hear revolutionary songs, programmes from the Chinese Peoples' Television Broadcasting Company and even international weather reports.

During those months, the streets were filled with people making desperate attempts to emulate Lei Feng. They kept their eyes peeled at all times, searching for a chance to perform a good deed. You only had to trip over a kerb, or carry a heavy-looking bag, and someone would charge forward to offer to help. And there was no chance of you ever losing anything. One day, a pencil dropped from my pocket, and before I knew it, three children rushed over, picked it up and said, 'Uncle, you've lost something,' then smiled sweetly and gave a Young Pioneer salute. I took the pencil from them and said, just as the newspaper told us to: 'Thank you, young comrades. You are real little Lei Fengs.'

'Don't mention it,' they piped in unison. 'We're only doing our duty.'

'Tell me, which school are you from? I would like to inform your headmaster of your exemplary behaviour.'

'A person who performs good deeds should never leave their name,' they chirped, then swung round and ran back to the end of the street to wait for their next prey, just like the Young Pioneers in the propaganda films.

We can all put up with taking the wrong road, but no one can bear reaching a dead end. When the survivor was alive, I was confused about everything – including him. I had lost my way. But after he died, I found I had nowhere to go. There was no hope left for me, nothing to look forward to. He had destroyed everything I believed in.

'Everything is decided for you by your superiors,' the dog said one day, 'what job you do, who you marry, how many children you have. You have no belief in your ability to control your destiny. Your lives are so dull and monotonous, if you weren't subjected to various trials and tribulations, you would never be strong enough to look death in the face.' The dog uttered these words on the roof terrace, his head framed by the azure sky. The fumes pouring from the chimney stacks behind him smelled like the sour steam that rises from fermenting tofu. Against the blue sky, the smoke was blindingly bright.

'I seem to have caught a cold,' the dog said. 'The breeze up here is bad for my health.' He had picked up that last phrase from me.

I still don't know how he died, though.

Sometimes I think he must have jumped from the roof. I imagine him darting across the terrace, then retreating to the edge as the old carpenter and the other two from the dog extermination brigade approached, followed by a pack of Young Pioneers brandishing spears and spades. He was either lassoed with a rope and dragged downstairs or beaten to death on the spot. His sharp claws and teeth couldn't protect him from them. Once they had decided he should die, there was nothing he could do.

My three-legged dog never liked the Young Pioneers. He said that after years of being told to sacrifice their lives to the Revolution, they turn into little hooligans who lack any sense of morality or common decency.

'They are children,' I said. 'We should forgive them. Childhood is sacred.'

He curled his lips and, glancing at the street below, said, 'See those children making fun of the blind man? Look at their ugly faces! If their teachers sent them out tomorrow to perform good deeds, they'd fight for the chance to grab the blind man's hand and help him across the road.'

Although their faces were a blur, I could see them racing across the blind man's path, performing karate moves they had picked up from some martial arts film. Then the dog asked: 'If you had to choose between me and a child, which one would you save?'

I couldn't answer. Even today I wouldn't be able to give an answer to that question. Naturally, I should put a human life before a dog's, but my feelings for the survivor far exceeded any I felt for those children in the street – they were even stronger than the feelings I had for my girlfriend. If those children were indeed responsible for the survivor's death, I know he wouldn't have put up a fight. He could have bitten off one of their legs had he wanted to, but he would have chosen to suffer in silence rather than cause them any harm.

When I returned from the conference, I made a thorough inspection of his body to try and find out the cause of his death. He reeked of formaldehyde, but there were no wounds on his skin. I patted him on the back and said, 'Look, they didn't hurt you at all! Why have you been lying to me in my dreams?'

A couple of weeks later, I returned to the workshop to speak to the carpenter. When I entered the room, he was nailing the skin of a Dongbei tiger onto a wooden frame. I asked him how the three-legged dog had died. He smiled amiably, and drawing the tiger's pelt across the frame, he said: 'A three-legged dog? I've seen a five-legged donkey and a five-legged bull. Ha ha! Those fifth legs were half the size of the others!' He roared with laughter, and made a lewd gesture above his groin.

I am convinced that Secretary Wang knows exactly how the dog died. I even suspect that he planned the murder himself. He is the museum's Party secretary, after all. Maybe he wanted to use this episode to test my loyalty to the Party. How could he not have known that I was keeping a dog on the terrace? Perhaps at first he decided to sit back and wait for me to confess my crime. But when he saw me commit mistake after mistake, he packed me off to a conference and got rid of the dog while I was away. When I returned from the trip, he convened an enlarged session of the Party cell, and encouraged the members to come forward and give their opinions on my relationship with the dog.

'The higher organs are putting me to the test,' I told the stuffed survivor the next time I visited him in the workshop. 'In the meeting before my trip, they asked if any comrades had something they wanted to reveal. I should have owned up about you there and then. You had the cheek to criticise my girlfriend for committing suicide, and then you go and die yourself!'

'Did you love her?' the stuffed survivor asked me suddenly. 'Don't you feel responsible for her death? Why was she so willing to throw her life away? How could you have let her go through with it? What was she trying to tell you?'

His questions left me speechless. I remembered the first time I met her, when I was chairman of the student union at school. If I hadn't got involved with her, I would probably have entered the Party that year. After I graduated from university, I was assigned a room in a staff dormitory block, and our friendship deepened. She would visit me every day and stay until ten at night, slipping out just before the security guard locked the front gates. In my darkened room, I would rest my head on her stomach and listen to the growling of her intestines. She lay down on my bed and gave herself to me. But even today, I don't know what I loved about her. She was a woman, my girlfriend, but had she been any other woman, would I have felt any different? How would I have reacted if my leaders hadn't agreed to our relationship? (She was still at drama school at the time and her lifestyle wasn't faultless.) Just before she died, her eyes were full of kindness and goodwill. I wondered whether she was hoping I would rush to her rescue.

'Then why didn't you try?' the survivor asked.

'I did jump to my feet at one point. But I had skived off a political meeting at work that day, and if news had got out that I wasn't ill at all, but had come to watch the performance, I would have got into terrible trouble. She knew very well that the higher organs were in the process of considering my application to join the Party.'

'You should be held responsible for her death.'

'No, my only responsibility is towards the Party,' I said, refusing to give in to him.

But there is one matter that still puzzles me, and that I suspect might have contributed to the dog's death. After I left for the conference, the dog somehow managed to climb to the top shelf and bring down those unhealthy books that only a select group of cadres are allowed to 'Read and Criticise'. They contain the reactionary thoughts of Nietzsche, Schopenhauer, Freud, and the much-discredited Hegel. The poor dog was completely unprepared for these ideas – he had never attended any political meetings, and he even held the reactionary opinion that Marxist-Leninism was out of date! Those books corrupted the minds of many poets and university students (including my girlfriend), driving them to a life of decadence, causing them to lose their normal sense of judgement. The dog must have squatted in the corner and read through every wretched book. If this did indeed happen, then I would certainly hold myself responsible for his death.

Now that he's gone, I have no use for the leftover bones in the cafeteria. But at mealtimes I still glance under the table looking for them, and when no one is watching, I kick them towards me, then wrap them up in a newspaper and take them home with me. This isn't a normal way to behave. Of course I know in my heart that the survivor is just a stuffed specimen now, but my feelings for him can't change overnight. In the evening, I wait for darkness to fall, then I walk to the edge of the terrace and toss the bones onto the streets below.

The terrace feels empty without him. His absence weighs heavily on my heart. My life has become disorderly, and my room is no longer as clean as it was when he was around. Mice scuttle across the metal joists on my ceiling now, and when they get tired they drop straight onto my bed. When the dog was alive, the mice only dared take their walks late at night when we were both asleep, and they never ventured far from the skirting board. Now large spiders climb between the rusty joists, sometimes winching themselves down to steal a piece of cake. The pollution outside seems to be getting worse by the day. A thick layer of dust hovers above the terrace, and the air smells of burnt plastic. At night, I close the door and stay inside. If I were to look through my telescope, I would be able to see all the stories taking place in the crowds below, but without the dog by my side, they would seem dull and meaningless. Besides, ever since the Campaign to Learn from Lei Feng was launched, the streets have become so well ordered, there's nothing much left to see.

Last week, I resolved to confess to my leaders all the unhealthy thoughts that have run through my mind over the past years, and promise that in the future I will align myself fully with the Party and the higher organs. In the enlarged session of the museum's Party cell meeting, Secretary Wang asked me and the other three colleagues whose Party membership was also under consideration to present self-criticisms about our thinking this year, and admit the mistakes we have committed against the Party. The young graduate confessed that she had read the pornographic novel *The Thoughts of a Young Girl*, and begged the higher organs to take disciplinary action against her. The old carpenter admitted that he'd constructed the top drawer of his wooden chest from a piece of state-owned hardboard, and he asked the leaders to accept his sincere apologies. Song Juhua from the finance department was still apologising for conceiving a child out of wedlock three years ago. When my turn came, I confessed to every reactionary opinion that either I or the dog had uttered. My mind was extraordinarily clear. I told them about every mistake we had committed, without omitting a single detail. I felt an immense wave of relief. The leaders remained silent throughout my speech, and when it came to an end they just said they would have to go away and look into the matter.

Since my confession, the sad look has vanished from the survivor's glass eyes. Although he is dead, his coat lives on, and will live on for ever. Never again will he have to hide himself from public view. He is a survivor who has seen through the red dust of the world. When he took part in the Beijing exhibition, he brought glory to our town. Everyone here started talking about my three-legged dog. People travelling here on business would hear about him as soon as they stepped off their train. Tourists would make special trips to visit him in the museum. His photo appeared in many magazines. I cut each one out and stuck them on my wall. Now at last he is able to show his face to the world. The crowds he so despised when he was alive are now his greatest admirers. Secretary Wang was so impressed by the carpenter's ability to create such a lifelike exhibit, he singled him out for praise on several occasions, and later awarded the survivor the title of 'Grade One Stuffed Animal'.

As dawn approaches, the writer's thoughts come to a sudden halt, like a generator that has run out of fuel. All the images that have raced through his head disappear into a vague mist. He has experienced these moments of calm before, when his mind temporarily disconnects from reality. But the calm he feels now seems different somehow. When he closes his eyes, the characters who have lived inside him so long seem like a lump of dough being pulled by invisible hands into a thousand white threads. He sees the threads pulled tighter and tighter, until suddenly they break into a million pieces and scatter into the night sky.

'I knew it would end like this,' the writer mutters to himself. 'Everything fades and dies. There's nothing I can do about it . . .'

The blood donor stares at the writer's shadow slanting on the wall behind. Now that the lights in the buildings outside have gone out, the lamps in the room seem brighter. The blood donor walks to the cassette player and turns the volume down. The writer rises to his feet, and ambles towards the toilet like a sleepwalker. As he listens to his urine splash into the bowl, he catches the smell of fish-head soup again. This time, the smell isn't wafting from his neighbour's kitchen, it's coming from inside his own body. Slowly he returns to his chair. Now that the alcohol has left their organs and evaporated through their orifices and pores, the two men look as dry as shrivelled oat flakes or lumps of burnt charcoal.

'My greatest achievement has been my ability to produce unending streams of AB blood,' the donor croaks, pulling his vest up and pointing to his heart. 'My blood has changed the course of my life. It has given it meaning.'

The writer's voice is now as soft as the Requiem Mass playing on the cassette player. Through the floating melody of the aria, the blood donor hears his friend say, 'Those people's lives were doomed from the start. Whatever ending I choose to give their stories won't change anything. I was just an onlooker, like that three-legged dog, hiding in the margins. You're the only one who'll ever hear these stories, but I'm the only one who can understand them. Only I know the pain that lies behind them.'

'My spirit may be weak, but my flesh is strong. That's why I fit into this town so well. But you will always be an outsider, lost in your illusions,' the blood donor says, in a condescending tone he has rarely used these past seven years.

'But those characters are real, they live in the same town as you and me. I may not know them very well, and they probably know even less about me. But I'm sure they exist. Or perhaps I've been dead for years, and those characters are just scraps of manuscript paper floating in some distant sewer.' The writer prods his skull. Then his eyes light up for a moment and he adds, 'I guarantee that my unwritten novel will have far more lasting value than any published book.'

'I too have many stories to tell,' the blood donor says. 'They're trapped inside me like water in a kettle. Maybe it's time I tried pouring them out . . .'

The writer stands up, rests his hands on his hips and says, 'My blood is worth nothing compared to that novel of mine.' Then he glances around the room and starts sniffing the air again. 'That fish-head soup must have been excellent,' he mumbles. 'I can smell it even now . . .'

The blood donor's cigarette is still alight. He now seems as deep in thought as a professional writer. He appears to be eager to set to work on some intellectual task. 'When we've no energy left to fight against this brutal world, we turn inwards and start harming ourselves,' he says, taking a last puff from his cigarette. He flings the stub to the ground, crushes it under the sole of his shoe, then walks next door to the writer's study, sits down on the chair and stares at the blank page on the desk.

In the last few minutes before dawn, the writer darts about his room like a maimed, wingless ladybird. Then, without saying a word, he opens his front door, shuts it quietly behind him, and disappears down the dark stairwell.

CPSIA information can be obtained
at www.ICGtesting.com
Printed in the USA
LVOW07s0227271217
560921LV00005B/462/P